Apache Spies

by Hollis Johnson

Green Ivy Publishing
1 Lincoln Centre
18W140 Butterfield Road
Suite 1500
Oakbrook Terrace IL 60181-4843
www.greenivybooks.com

ISBN: 978-1-945379-09-3

Chapter 1

February 1980. Stress has a different effect on everyone. Some people hate it. A rare few love it, and those are the ones who pass tier one special operations training. No matter the country, the philosophy of special operations forces training is the same—stress the potential candidates to the point where the body can no longer function unless the mind is enjoying every second of the training. This theory seems draconian in Western society, where discipline plays second fiddle to someone's sensitivity. Ironically, Great Britain is known throughout the world as being at the forefront special operations because they were able cast a side political correctness. The 22nd Special Air Service Regiment doesn't just live and breathe this philosophy; they conceived it. It is a philosophy that has held up to empirical research and forty years of deployments. They will never compromise—even when it comes to women.

When Helen Masters was nine years old, she lost her father, who was an American soldier in Vietnam during the Tet Offensive in 1969. She did not see her father often, except for the annual trip to Dallas, Texas, where her grandparents lived. Helen loved traveling and spending time with her grandparents, Paul and Rita—Gram and Grammy as Helen called them. Rita was a full-blooded Apache, and she and Helen could have passed for mother and daughter. Both had dark, long hair and strong athletic frames, which was why Helen played baseball with her cousins and friends more than she played with dolls. Paul always said jokingly that the intensity of their stares could burn a hole through a safe, though he never said it when Rita was around.

After 1969, visits became less frequent and were replaced with the occasional phone call. Barbara, Helen's mother, was worried that the southwestern environment—particularly Rita—was not teaching Helen to become a lady. When Helen came back from America in 1970, Barbara was curious to know about her daughter's vocation and what she had learned over the summer. Much to Barbara's dismay, Helen broke into a full Apache ceremonial song, and enough was enough.

Barbara Simon had met Todd Masters in the fall of 1959 while she was studying medicine at the University of Georgia on a student exchange program. Todd was stationed nearby at Fort Benning, finishing up airborne training, and he attended the annual American football game between Auburn University and Georgia Bulldogs. Todd, a huge college football fan, had road-tripped with a couple of buddies 160 miles north to Athens, Georgia. Barbara didn't like or understand the appeal of the contest. It seemed like an excuse for morons to beat the hell out of each other. She felt that maybe if the students paid more attention to the disgraceful way the Negros were being treated, maybe sports that promoted violence would not resonate so well. But the atmosphere at local college bars after the game were fun and good for blowing off steam. After the hometown Bulldogs won 21–14, the festive attitude turned up a notch. Since she was a pretty blonde with light brown eyes, it didn't take long before she caught Todd's eye.

Helen thought that Brecon Beacons and the Elan Valley looked like something from a science fiction movie, cold and unyielding. The North Atlantic wind whipped in a swirling fashion around the hills and mountains. This made navigating to different checkpoints frustrating. After thirty days navigating mountainous terrain with very little food and even less sleep, she was just happy to have survived the first round known as selection. It was the SAS version of a job interview, a seven-month audition to see if a candidate was worthy to be trained. Ninety percent wouldn't make it; many would just quit, or die if they were unlucky. The fact that Helen was underestimated because she was the only woman there was an advantage. She had no expectations, which just made her work harder.

Helen Masters was born in London on the twenty-fifth of August 1960. Her mother and father were never married because of the transient nature of their relationship. Barbara was on a student visa and had to return home in May. Todd was in the United States Army. But their love and respect for one another was unshakable. Of course, Barbara's parents were less than pleased. They had big dreams for their daughter, and getting pregnant before finishing medical school was not one of them. Todd's family was more upset by the fact they would see the new member of the family maybe once a year.

Raised primarily by her grandmother Ida "Nana" Simon while Barbara completed school, Helen grew up healthy and strong. Bill Simon died of a heart attack 1967 but left a successful shipping business and sizeable life insurance policy to provide for his family. Throughout the rest of her childhood, Helen excelled at academics and athletics, which fostered an early advancement to college.

Walking the hallowed halls of Cambridge University was intimidating for most mature first-year students, but for a fifteen-year-old, it could be a disaster. But Helen handled herself well, even when it came to boys. The age difference was obviously not only a moral problem but a legal one. There were advances from the more adolescent male members of the student body who were trying to impress their friends. This was where Grammy's influence bore fruit. She had taught her granddaughter how to defend herself the Apache way. The rumors spread fast about the sweet young thing who, if provoked, would break fingers, punch a man's lights out, and use a fork in a way that could only be described as a man's worst nightmare.

Now the plan was simple—four years of college to graduate, with honors of course. Get a medical school scholarship, graduate, become a doctor, marry well, have children, and live happily ever after. But Helen had another plan—to prove that she was capable of outperforming any man, anytime, anywhere. Naturally, this goal could be a real turnoff for the opposite sex. The male-dominated world, with Neanderthal thinking, suggested that men could do anything, whereas women should be satisfied with domestic responsibilities. Many of Helen's dates were prematurely ended, and even more potential boyfriends were scared away.

So, instead of continuing her education after college and taking a residency at a prestigious hospital somewhere abroad, Helen decided to accept an offer to join the secret intelligence service, or MI6. Helen's training began at Fort Monckton about two hundred miles west of London. The rigorous training was enjoyable in a perverted sort of way. She found out very quickly that spy craft was not for everyone. Because of a high failure rate and individual lack of self-discipline, the size of her class was cut by 66 percent in a matter of months. But, through it all, Helen excelled, especially at marksmanship.

In 1979, a year into training, she received horrible news. Her mother had been diagnosed with breast cancer.

A large lump had been found near Dr. Barbara Simon's right armpit. Apparently, she had written it off as an ingrown hair due to shaving. This proved, once again, that doctors make the worst patients. The cancer was aggressive and spread rapidly to her lungs. Barbara was a heavy smoker, which was normal for someone of her generation. Things like minimum age requirements, warning labels, and education did not materialize until the 1970s. Within weeks, Dr. Simon had succumbed to the disease. The funeral was held at St. Michael's, a small hometown church in Brighton, where more friends than family showed. Barbara came from a long line of only children, which was why her English family was so small. Helen had enjoyed her time in Dallas playing with all of her cousins because it was something she did not experience at home.

As good as Helen felt at graduating from MI6 training, she felt equally disappointed, if not more so, at finding that intelligence work was 90 percent administrative. It was a lot like working for a bank or any other corporation, including mundane responsibilities like typing, filing, and accounting. So, when word got out that the prime minister and defense minister had made a Job-like bet on whether or not a woman could pass SAS selection and also qualify as a team member, Helen was the first volunteer.

Before the trucks carrying what was left of two hundred candidates had stopped, Helen awoke to get a quick head count. There were not more than thirty left. She felt pity for the poor bastards who'd injured themselves and screamed for help, which only came at the earliest convenience of the directing staff or DS. As a medical professional, Helen exerted every ounce of her will to refrain from giving assistance to the fallen. When the trucks' brakes screeched to a halt, all the DS membership started yelling military clichés like "drop your cocks and grab your socks" or "you people move slower than old people fuck." Helen found all this humorous. How would one know the speed in which elderly people had sex? Was this some sort of unofficial Olympic event, or maybe the DS staff member who uttered the phase was revealing his own personal sexual proclivity. When Command Sergeant Major Winston appeared from his barracks, all yelling and movement ceased.

CSM Morris Winston was celebrating his forty-five-year anniversary, forty-two in the regiment, by tormenting a few wet noses. The sergeant major's stare was penetrating. He made sure he locked eyes with each of them before he spoke in his hard Scotsman accent.

"OK, I see we couldn't kill or make all of you quit, and that really pisses me off. Personally, I think the lot of ya are a waste of the crown's money. So ya fucks get all expenses paid vacation to the jungles of Belize." Winston turned slowly, caught Helen's gaze, and continued with a grin. "There are things in the jungle that will eatcha alive. You might want to consider that anybody can quit anytime, and save yourself."

Winston turned the detail over to the senior DS and disappeared back into the barracks. The DS started to shout orders in between clichés. Helen held her anger in because, even though she technically outranked him (she was officially a second lieutenant) and his comments made have crossed the line, this was not the Army. Within the SAS, rank was earned not given. Winston was a living legend, and she was a nobody. Besides, she had bigger fish to fry—two months of jungle training in Central America. After that, if she was lucky, two months of desert training in northern Africa. Cheers.

Chapter 2

At 2:00 a.m. on Thursday, June 12, a dark blue van drove very slowly down the upper-middle-class neighborhood of Venice Beach, California, and pulled to a stop. Venice Beach was one of the last remnants of the hippie culture, and unfortunately, drugs and crime had slowly overtaken people whose basic philosophy was peaceful enlightenment. The two occupants of the van marked Southland Plumbing Company were anything but that. It was a stolen van with a legitimate name so if a nosy, or more likely bored, cop started to ask questions, there was a plausible excuse. Someone was always in need of emergency plumbing services, especially in this area where the business activity on and near Pacific Coast Highway was high. These were the kind of details that Phillipe Rainbird—or Lil Trace, as he was called on the streets—always took into account. He was a good-looking black male with the physique of an athlete. At the tender age of seventeen, he had learned a wealth of knowledge while embarking on a highly successful criminal run in the last year. But this job was different; it was a paid assassination.

When most teenagers were knocking over the occasional liquor store or other high-risk low-payout venture, Phillipe was robbing banks and armored cars, and moving major weight in marijuana. And yes, he also had to hurt or kill people, but only as a last resort. He wanted money, and if a person helped him get it, cool. But, to anyone who stole from him or hurt family and friends, he showed no mercy. The difference between Phillipe and some wild-ass gangbanger was self-control and intelligence. He did nothing without thinking the situation through.

Phillipe Rainbird was born on the fifth of March 1962 to William and Mary, high school sweethearts. His sister Patricia was two years his senior. They lived in an unincorporated area of south Los Angeles called Athens. Both Phillipe and Pat had excelled at school, which made them eligible for advanced studies. When William and Mary decided to divorce, it was difficult for the kids. William, like most black men of his era, was tormented by overt racism, and this led to excessive drinking and erratic behavior. He was never physically abusive, but he felt powerless against a society that seemed to want nothing more than to watch a black man fail.

After the divorce, money was scarce, but Mary managed by selling Avon and Tupperware products, along with working her regular job at the gas company. William's truck driving kept him away for long periods, and this was a recipe for disaster. Predators have an uncanny ability to detect weakness, no matter how small. Ghetto predators are no different. They sensed that Pat was vulnerable but could not have been further from the truth. Since the age of seven, Phillipe had been spending that last part of summer, after little league was over, with his granddad. Goya Rainbird was the last surviving full-blooded relative of Geronimo, and he embraced all of the knowledge bestowed on him by his parents. His parents had escaped from relocation in Florida and made their way to Yazoo County, Mississippi, where they bought land. Cotton was the cash crop of choice, so they applied themselves and learned quickly, but they never forgot their ways, the ways of the Chiricahua Apache, which they passed on to their seven children.

Granddad taught Phillipe the importance of education and patience. He emphasized agricultural science, land navigation, and hunting. They both would spend weeks living off the land and tracking game. Goya treasured his time with his grandson, which compensated in a way for his not being there for his own sons. The guilt that granddad felt was understandable because, when his sons were young, granddad had been part of the World War II Tuskegee Airmen program, as instructor. During World War I while attending Alcorn State, Goya had been recruited by the Royal Canadian Air Force. There was a shortage of qualified applicants in Canada, so the Canadians felt that the Americans could provide the necessary manpower. It was a perfect opportunity, especially since nonwhites were not allowed to fly planes in the United States military. Goya couldn't resist, though his mother was displeased, to say the least. Once she stopped yelling, she tried to beat him with a broom. She had already buried a husband and a daughter, and the thought of losing her youngest was unbearable.

Goya told stories about flying reconnaissance missions over France. He would describe how beautiful France looked from the air, but only when the enemy wasn't shooting at him. When asked if he had seen the Red Baron, his reply was always the same. "Reconnaissance planes had no guns, so I stayed far away from that crazy white man."

So, when the war department asked if Goya would be interested in Eleanor Roosevelt's pet project at Tuskegee University, he said yes. By now his mother had passed on, but his wife, Rose, was up to the challenge of shoving that broom up his ass. Rose, a smart and ambitious Negro woman, didn't want her two young sons to be orphans. Even though Alabama wasn't that far away, Rosie had become disenchanted with farm life and taking care of two small children alone. She had had enough, so she packed up, and the three of them moved to Los Angeles, California. Rosie got a job as a janitor at a local hospital and as a part-time maid on the weekends.

Goya didn't know what had happened until he came home on leave.

Goya and Rosie soon agreed to divorce, which meant she liked LA too much to come back. Granddad tried to act as if the circumstances had no effect on him by keeping busy with the farm, singing at church, and using his tracking skills to hunt escaped convicts for the state of Mississippi. This ate away at him for two decades until Phillipe's first visit.

Phillipe's mind was always active, but tonight it was in overdrive going over the scouting and planning. This was not a street hit or a stupid drive-by. The people, or "targets," in question were state witnesses for the Los Angeles district attorney's office. The defendants were the infamous Strong family, and at top of the list was Tracy "Big Trace" Strong, the leader of the family. He was Phillipe's mentor and his namesake.

They had met when Phillipe was nine, before the Strong family went big time, normal Saturday afternoon kids playing at the local park. Big Trace and crew were "holding things down," meaning they were niggas just standing around doing nothing. When the ice cream man made his regular visit, all the kids rushed the truck. But Teddy "Bear" Smith, the main enforcer of the family, pushed his way to the front and announced, "If any y'all want ice cream, buy me some!" Not wanting feel the Bear's wrath, all the kids scattered except one. Phillipe stood his ground and politely said, "Please move." The Bear was a high school football phenom—six feet three inches, 240 pounds. College scouts were all over him until they discovered he was illiterate. In the 1970s, this wasn't a big issue, but he was an absolute fool, with a long criminal history and drug abuse.

Bear told Phillipe, "Little nigga, gimme some money before I fuck you up!" But Phillipe looked in his eyes and calmly said, "Nigga, suck my dick." Before Bear could smack the shit out Phillipe, Big Trace stepped in and told Bear to back down and stop messing with little kids.

From that moment on, Trace was the big brother Phillipe had never had. And now the Bear held a grudge, and at every opportunity would give Phillipe shit. Big Trace knew Phillipe was a straight A student, so he encouraged him and let him run errands, legal and illegal. This mentoring prompted the nickname Lil Trace. It all came to a head with Bear when Phillipe turned twelve, once again over money. Lunch runs were the most common job. Phillipe would take orders and money, ride his bike to Steven's Burgers. He never forgot an order or mishandled the money. Phillipe and Pat both had photographic memories, like Dad. Bear was in rare form that day, binge drinking and sniffing heroin. He was slipping, becoming more of a liability and insecure about his position within the family. So he decided pick on Phillipe, disputing his change. The argument escalated into an all-out fight between a twelve-year-old kid and a twenty-one-year-old punk, with the obvious outcome being that Philippe was put in the hospital for several weeks. When questioned by the police as to who assaulted him, Phillipe said that he had fallen down. Willie and Mary knew who the possible assailant was but couldn't agree on a course of action. They argued intensely for days but found no resolution. On the other hand, Phillipe knew what he wanted to do and exactly what he needed to do. Now Phillipe had a grudge.

After a while, things returned to normal. Phillipe's wounds healed. He returned to school and the boy scouts, and as far as his parents were concerned, the matter was closed. No permanent damage had been done, and boys will be boys. But under no circumstances was Phillipe or his sister ever to go near that damn park from now to the end of time. No problem. Phillipe had work to do, like assessing himself and the situation. He had made many mistakes in his confrontation with Bear—for instance, letting him get too close. With no ability for Phillipe to maneuver, Bear's massive size had negated Phillipe's speed. And frankly, Phillipe had been intimidated, and this fear had led to hesitation. So he started taking jujitsu classes two hours a day after school, six days a week. The owner of the school was also a locksmith, and Phillipe would pay for lessons by cleaning up both the shop and the dojo. He even learned how to make keys and work and pick different types of locks. Cool.

Three years passed. Phillipe grew taller, stronger, and—more importantly—smarter. On the other hand, Bear's weight ballooned to over three hundred pounds, he was now was a full-blown alcoholic, and he was still a fool "holding down" the same park bench since he was thirteen. Phillipe knew the time was right, but he also knew Bear had a gun.

It was the summer before Phillipe started high school when he went back to the park for the first time in three years, the local park named Helen Keller. The day was a carbon copy of the last time. There were lots of kids, picnics, baseball games, and ice cream trucks. By now, the Strong family was big time—no more hanging out at the park, and most of them had apartments and houses. Some had wives and kids. Obviously, Bear didn't get the memo, or he was just living in the past. Phillipe carefully walked toward Bear, smiling to not arouse suspicion. He knew it wouldn't take much conversation to piss Bear off. Bear had bragged for three years about his superhuman exploits over a twelve-year-old, so just the audacity of Phillipe showing up at his park drove him crazy. Lil Trace never said a word.

Bear's first predictable reaction was to jump up quickly to intimidate. But the weight and alcohol fucked with his equilibrium. He was off balance from the get-go, and Phillipe wasted time with several strikes to Bear's face and knees. Blood oozed from his nose and mouth. In a second predictable move, he extended his right hand toward Phillipe, a bone-headed attempt to put hands on Phillipe or to gain balance. Big mistake. Phillipe knew Bear was right handed and kept the .357 Magnum on his right side. There was no way his fat ass could get to it, so Phillipe grabbed his arm and broke it at the elbow and wrist. Using Bear's weight against him, Phillipe threw him into the park bench he was "holding down." As luck would have it, the .357 fell out of Bear's pocket near his left hand. A crowd of approving bystanders cheered Phillipe on prematurely. Bear willed himself toward the pistol. He could not see Phillipe clearly, so the fuckin' asshole pointed the Magnum at the crowd. Phillipe yelled "GUN!" Bear shot five times into the crowd. Fortunately no one was hit, but mayhem ensued.

By the time Bear struggled to his feet, everyone was running for cover. He couldn't find that lil punk muthafucka, and both knees were damaged and throbbed with pain. This further enraged him, though Phillipe was standing right behind him near the swimming pool building. Unknown to Bear, the Los Angeles County Sheriff Department had responded, and deputies were walking cautiously toward the armed suspect when Phillipe appeared and shouted, "Hey!"

Bear saw Phillipe and raised his pistol, forgetting that he had only one bullet left. He fired at the general direction of the cops, and they opened fire. Bear took three bullets to the upper body, but they hit nothing but fat. Unfortunately, Bear survived and got fifteen years. Phillipe had gotten revenge but pissed off Big Trace. He'd attacked one of his boys. Sure,

Bear was a drunk and stupid, but it was the principle. If he allowed Phillipe to slide, it would undermine his leadership.

So, Big Trace confronted Phillipe one on one. His first comment set the tone. "Man, what the fuck is wrong with you?"

Phillipe's best answer was to say nothing. This was a lecture, not a conversation. Big continued, " Didn't I tell yo black ass not to go to the park ever? And you costin' me money. You put my boy in a coma."

There it is, Phillipe thought. No matter what came out of his mouth about disobedience or Bear's health, priority number one was money. Greed was his weakness, and that's what Phillipe would exploit. Before Big could continue, Phillipe asked, "How much do I owe you?"

Big Trace was surprised that Phillipe would say anything, and confused about whether he was serious or this was a deflection tactic. Big called his bluff, saying, "You can't count that high. Besides, your mama would cut me a new asshole if you worked for me." The doors of opportunities had just opened.

Phillipe's plan was clever. He'd run his own crew like a contracting service. The only people who would know about the accord were Big and Phillipe. Now Big wanted an open-ended deal with no expiration. Phillipe said, "Six months," but Big indicated that he was negotiating from strength—in other words, he could just kill him.

Phillipe replied, "Then you might as well kill me, because I'm going to college in three years. It's one year or fuck it."

Big was more and more impressed with this young

man and felt pride that he was his namesake. So Big agreed and put him to work immediately. Transportation and other "things."

Phillipe's crew stayed busy, so the year went quickly. The agreement was fulfilled, but the crew continued to work their own hustle, whatever and whenever they could. In Phillipe's senior year of high school, he realized that college wasn't for him. Whether for maturity or finances or both, he decided to join the military. Since cash was king, the crew cranked it up a notch to include bank and armored car robberies.

By now, Phillipe's crew consisted of Jack, a fellow Apache who was muscle with a brain, and the Landon brothers, good thieves who would never back down from a fight, especially with each other. One of Phillipe's partners was Jennifer Parker—the other passenger in the van—an Italian girl with sandy brown hair and a great figure. Now, Jen's good looks were deceiving, which was why she was in the van. Policemen tended to be more sympathetic toward white women who were lost or confused. The damsel in distress worked every time. And if by chance the police wanted to know "who's the nigger in the back," she could subtly say "He's one of the people who work for my daddy's company, and my daddy is sick. I must have taken the wrong turn. I'm just driving the night crew to jobs to make sure nothing gets stolen." Having been duped, the officer would not only help with directions but issue a stern warning to the black guy to behave himself. And that's why Phillipe loved her.

Surprisingly, one day the word in the neighborhood was that Bear had gotten out early. Allegedly, his lawyer got him out on a technicality, which didn't seem right. But Phillipe was his own person, and as long as Bear didn't try any shit, as far as Phillipe was concerned, they were even.

But still, out in only three years after shooting at the police with a hundred witnesses just didn't seem right. One day, Phillipe came home from school to find Bear standing outside his house talking to his sister. Phillipe always carried switchblade and prepared himself, walking cautiously. Bear turned toward him, smiled, and said, "Check out this lil muthafucka. You think you a man, nigga?"

Phillipe looked at his sister and said, "Go in the house and lock the door."

Bear cut in with, "Ah, baby, you got me all wrong. I came by to say what's up. It ain't like that no mo!"

Phillipe was getting a bad vibe. Bear laughing and shooting the shit with him? Granted, Bear looked better than the last time Phillipe had seen him, but this was strange.

Bear continued. "I heard you the man now. Got yo own crew, you lil hustlin' muthafucka!"

Questions? Phillipe's paranoia hit the ceiling, and he went into complete denial mode. "Nah, man. Don't know what you're talking about."

Bear tried hard to prime the conversational pump, but Phillipe stuck to his guns of denial. Bear finally gave up, his brain probably overheated. He told Phillipe that he'd see him around. He said, "Tell that fine ass sister of yours give me a call. Ha ha ha!"

Phillipe realize two things that day. First, Bear was a snitch. Second, he had no choice but to kill Bear. Phillipe had sacrificed his life and education to secure his family's financial future. His family could not afford to send their children to college. And he could not sit in some dorm room while his family struggled. So he decided that after graduation he would join the United States Navy and become a Seabee. He would do a four-year tour and pay his own way through college. But Phillipe could not leave knowing Bear was chasing his sister. So Phillipe and the crew made it a priority to prove Bear was a snitch.

Jen followed Bear's dopehead girlfriend, Sophie Doucette, around. Everything seemed normal until Sophie left her house and caught several buses. Why would she leave a brand-new Cadillac in the driveway? Her destination was Denny's restaurant on Sunset Boulevard. Sophie met with a woman in her late thirties or early forties who look like a librarian. Jen reached for her camera and zoomed in. The camera shuttered several exposures. "This doesn't look good," Jen thought to herself.

Once the pictures were developed, Big took them to his contact, one of his lawyers, who gave them a quick glance and immediately recognized the librarian as an assistant district attorney! Whether or not Bear knew mattered no longer.

Jennifer was the daughter of a Philadelphia mafia boss named Nicky "The Crowbar" Pozzi. She used her mother's maiden name because she had been born out of wedlock. Old Nicky never denied her anything, especially his love. But Crowbar had a family, and he didn't believe in divorce, so he moved Jenn and her mom, Cindy, to Phoenix, Arizona. Phillipe met Jenn during a California state invitational swim and diving meet at Cerritos College. A mutual friend introduced them. She was the star at the hundred-meter freestyle. Phillipe's ten-meter diving was excellent, and the two of them hit it off immediately. Jenn thought Phillipe was a renegade after she found out about his "occupation," and that served as an aphrodisiac. And she wanted in—not for money but for the rush.

After Big discovered there was a rat in the click, he immediately left town. He left orders with Phillipe to get that punk bitch. He also ordered a $25,000 bounty on Bear's head, and he wanted to be brutal. Sophie was a bonus. Big said, "I'm not paying for that white bitch. I just never liked that ho."

Phillipe negotiated ten grand up front, the rest when the job was completed. That way it would decrease the chances that Big would try to "save" money. The rest of the Strong family went in different directions. When Bear got up the next morning and retrieved the paper, there was a dead rat inside, and he knew that it was over. He ran inside to call the DA. The cops rushed over, secured the area, and brought them to a safe house in Venice Beach. Following standard operating procedures, they rounded up every colored person, including Mexicans and Japanese, to locate Big's crew. This, to say the least, was futile. Bear was the one person dumb enough to drop a dime on Big.

Phillipe and Jenn went over the plan one last time. They knew the location, which had been found by one of Big's friends who worked at the phone company. Sophie was stupid and predictable. She called her rich Orange County daddy once a week. She was located by a simple reverse trace to the phone booth she used. The crew alternated, following her to and from the phone booth every Friday. She had just one undercover cop escort. Sophie had a jones for Chinese food, so like clockwork, on the way back to the safe house, she would as stop at Tin Sing restaurant and pick up takeout.

Two two-man rotating plainclothes teams were pulling twenty-four-hour surveillance. They parked in front of the house in an unmarked car. And they would sometimes doze off. Great.

Bear and Sophie would drink, party, and fight. The cops didn't care as long as they were alive and the neighbors weren't complaining. The best approach was the back door through the neighbor's backyard. Problem: They had two Dobermans. Solution: Two pounds of ground beef for a couple of weeks. The dogs got accustomed to the nightly visit, and everyone became best buddies. The dog owners were being "entertained" tonight by Apache Jack. He'd broken into the house and tied them up. Jack's other responsibility was to stay in radio contact with the rest of the team. The Landon brothers were backup, in a car a block away. Showtime.

Phillipe exited the van moving swiftly and quietly like Granddad taught him, with no wasted motion. He approached the house carrying a black backpack. The little doggies were so happy to see the hamburger Santa Claus, they started to piss and fight over who would get loved first. Tonight the dogs got a special treat—four pounds of meat laced with sleeping pills. While the dogs ate, Jack signaled that everything was OK. In thirty seconds, the dobermans had finished their meal. Phillipe carefully opened the gate and gave each dog a pat on the head. He made it across the backyard, but not too fast. He negotiated the five-foot-high chain link fence in one easy jump. The back door was on the north wall of the kitchen, and east of that was a window. Phillipe peeked in and saw Bear sleeping. A fifth of Smirnoff, about three quarters emptied, lay across his lap. Good news: He was at least inebriated. Bad news: He was unpredictable because no one spends three years in San Quentin state penitentiary and comes out the same person.

Phillipe heard the doggies whimper and groan. The sleeping pills must be kicking in, and that should keep them quiet. He kneeled down, took off the pack, and opened it. Inside there was a homemade slim-jim—basically a thin piece of metal with grooves and a hook on the end. This was to work the lock of the wooden screen door. Also in the pack was a can of WD-40. A couple of well-placed squirts and there would be no squeaky doors. The jim slipped in easy between the door and frame. A single click opened it. Phillipe went into the pack again and retrieved a small leather case. Inside was his lock pick set. He worked both locks with great efficiency. Before he opened the door, he looked around. Jack gave a signal with his lighter that the coast was clear. Phillipe slowly turned the doorknob. The door cracked open, and he stopped to get the WD-40. The hinges had paint all over them, which made the WD-40 even more important. Phillipe continued slowly to prevent noise, and the door moved.

Phillipe looked around. The house, which was powder blue with white trim and had three bedrooms, was actually quite nice. The kitchen was spacious with vintage 1950s appliances and Spanish tile floors. He walked without noise into the living room. The pine hardwood floors were dusty, and the whole house reeked of marijuana. Phillipe peeked around the corner into the den where Bear lay passed out. Sophie was upstairs asleep with the television blaring. Phillipe put the pack down and pulled out a homemade garrote, strung with piano wire.

Bear's big ass was in a recliner that was way too small for him, snoring loudly. Phillipe's approach was smooth and silent. He wrapped the garrote around Bear's neck. In one swift, violent move, Phillipe tighten the wire and lifted Bear slightly out of the seat. Bear's reaction was confusion and panic, and once he realized that he wasn't dreaming, he started to fight. The piano wire was not only causing him to suffocate, but it was also cutting into both carotid arteries. Even at half speed, Bear was a load, and Phillipe could barely hang on. Trying to yell out, Bear started to gasp for air. Phillipe's well-conditioned muscles were screaming for a break, but he could not stop to give an inch. Bear fell down to one knee, Phillipe gave one last surge strength, blood poured, and Bear's body shook. There was a cough and gurgling sounds, and then Bear's body went limp.

Phillipe gathered himself quickly, leaving the garrote around Bear's neck. He moved silently to the backpack. There was a milk container filled with gasoline, and he poured it all over Bear. He reached in and got a small screwdriver, some fishline, and a WP grenade. WP was short for white phosphorus, an incendiary device known as "Willie Pete." Phillipe checked to make sure that the cops were still being cops—reading or sleeping or whatever. He began to rig the grenade to the guardrail on the stairs with a little duct tape. He placed a small Phillips screw in the baseboard and tied the fishline across the stairs to the pin of the grenade. He did a quick check to make sure everything was copacetic, then immediately went to the kitchen behind the stove. Inside of the pack was a pair of channel-lock pliers. He loosened the coupling, and the gas came hissing out. Brutal? You goddamn right!

The most dangerous parts of Phillipe's plan were the end game, escape, and alibis. He exited the house quietly and patiently waited for Jack's OK signal. Once Phillipe received the all-is-well sign—a quick flash of flame in the back kitchen window—he moved to the chain link fence, where he saw his fur-covered buddies lying peacefully. Quietly, he opened the back door and closed it behind himself. He checked the corner of the house to make sure everything was clear. By this time, the doggies were staggering to their feet. Phillipe jumped the fence easily and landed softly. He walked with purpose to the other side of the yard, the dogs trying to keep up. Before leaving, he patted the good doggies on their heads. Jack locked the homeowners in bathroom, just in case they had to go potty, and radioed the signal to be picked up. Phillipe opened and closed the gate at the same time that Jack was coming out of the house. Both acknowledged one another. Jack turned left and went west; Phillipe went east. When Phillipe was a block away, Jenn, in the plumber's van, slowed and allowed him to get in.

Jack walked toward the beach, where there was a diagonal parking lot, put in for some business fronts. A motorcycle, which Jack had stolen earlier in the day, had a storage compartment. Inside was a pair of Nike Cortez shoes. He took off his dark-colored sweat suit, boots, and gloves. He threw all of it into a trash bin. Underneath was a pair of jeans and a Polo shirt. Jack slipped on the pair of Nikes and put on the helmet. The bike cranked over and sped away, heading south on Lincoln Boulevard. After getting the word on the radio, the Landon brothers went east on Venice Boulevard to get on the 10 freeway.

The Landons went on vacation to Las Vegas. Of course, being out of town before Bear was discovered wasn't a bad idea. Jack's destination was Arizona, by way of Los Angeles International Airport, or LAX. This was where Jack had stolen the bike. He parked the motorcycle exactly where he had "found" it and jumped on the Hertz rental car twenty-four-hour shuttle. Hertz was located on Aviation Boulevard and Arbor Vitae Street. He exited the bus and walked briskly out of the gate. Jack's jeep was parked in the adjacent neighborhood.

Jenn drove the van north on Sepulveda. Phillipe was busy changing clothes. Jenn already had prepped the van by lining the entire back with Visqueen, a thick construction-grade plastic drop cloth. All of Phillipe's clothes were covered in blood. He undressed and rolled up the Visqueen. He wiped himself down with some wet napkins and put on a brown Adidas warm-up suit. Jenn was heading north on the 405 freeway, and she got off on Roscoe. At this point, Phillipe was busy getting ready to dump the van. A couple of turns, and they were in a vacant lot. Both knew what needed to be done. Jenn opened the gas tank and shoved a towel in until only twelve inches hung out. Phillipe positioned three one-gallon milk containers filled with gasoline in the cargo bay. He took out one more WP grenade, and leaving the back door open, he pulled the pin and tossed it in.

Phillipe and Jenn walked away, and five seconds later, there was a blinding light and smoke. The grenade went from zero to five thousand degrees, instantly burning and melting all the milk containers. Thirty seconds later, this created a raging fire. In ninety seconds, the towel caught fire and transferred it to the gas tank.

A huge explosion echoed though the quiet industrial area. Meanwhile, Phillipe and Jenn were a block away in her VW bus. They never spoke or looked back. The ride back to Phillipe's house was a time for contemplating the future. Jenn thought about returning to college. She wasn't sure if she wanted to go back to Arizona State University. Maybe she could transfer to Cal State Fullerton. They had a good swim team. Besides, the weather in Los Angeles was so much better than in Arizona. Phillipe's focus was on the fact that Big owed him $15,000, and the entire crew knew Big had given the order. Big could kill them all, tie up loose ends, and save money in the process. That was one reason the Landon brothers went to Vegas. Big and his entourage were staying at MGM Grand casino so they could watch Big's ass.

Danny and Sammy Landon were fraternal twins. Their father had committed suicide in their senior year of high school. Mr. Landon shot himself in his car after being laid off from Northrop. Danny and Sammy found him, and it changed everything. Mrs. Landon immersed herself in work and church, and the boys decided they needed to make some money to help out. They were already stealing and knew Moms wouldn't take their "sin" money, so they joined the Marine Corps. After four years in the military, they had learned how to steal and get away with it.

Phillipe and Jenn slowly pulled in front of the Rainbird house and parked behind Phillipe's VW Beetle. He looked at his watch. It was 4:05 a.m. He said flatly, "You know Big will probably try to kill us."

Jenn smiled and replied, "The operative word is try."

Phillipe turned toward her and looked into her eyes to emphasize his point and said, "I don't mean you. You're the Crowbar's daughter. Touching you would cause a shit storm." He paused for a moment and continued. "Now that I think about it, Crowbar will fuck me up real bad if he knew about all the shit we pulled this last year."

Jenn put her hand on his crotch and gently massaged his dick until he began to swell. She leaned toward his ear whispering, "I won't tell if you don't."

Phillipe looked at his watch again. It was 4:08 a.m. He said, "Baby, I got to get into the house. I graduate high school this morning. If I'm late, Moms will kick my ass!"

Jenn wasn't listening. She was horny, and she didn't

give a shit. They went to the back of the bus and started to go at it. While taking off Phillipe's pants, Jenn passionately said, "A little graduation pussy can't hurt!" and Phillipe thought to himself, "Muthafuckin' right!"

■ Chapter 3 ■

June twelfth, 5:00 a.m. In the jungle, there was always a sound to indicate what was going on, day or night, which heightens one's awareness. The noise of a twig snapping, based on the tone, can distinguish between a human or an animal. Mountain Pine Ridge Training Area, located southwest of Belmopan, Cayo, Belize, was where phase two of SAS selection was conducted. Helen Masters was barely halfway through jungle training, which included sixty days of four-man patrols, carrying a forty-pound Bergen (or rucksack), and hiking twenty kilometers a day. The two biggest problems Helen had was keeping her shite dry and not being violated by every bug and snake looking for a warm place to call its own. She was under a lean-to preparing to go on watch, using all the proper techniques and discipline to keep her feet dry. Wet feet inside boots equaled jungle rot, basically a flesh-eating fungus. Helen put her boots and rain cammies on and ventured out into the driving rain.

She was assigned the northeast perimeter, and the team was standing two on/two off. The shifts were in four-hour intervals. She was relieving Smithfield, a nice fellow as far as candidates go. There wasn't a lot of time for socializing, and the training started out being very individualized. There had been no team building until now, but due to fatigue and the miserable conditions, no one had the extra strength to find out what they liked or disliked about another person. This strategy was by design. Humans are foolish when they are comfortable, and the strategy produced a change in normal behavior patterns. Complex psychological issues such as racial and gender biases become unimportant compared to survival.

Helen walked to the general vicinity, but she didn't see Smithfield. After waiting a few moments, she activated her throat microphone. The radio broke squelch. "One, this is four. What's your locale?" Simultaneously, she felt a hand on her shoulder. With lightning speed, she elbowed the assailant in the groin and face. Using his body weight against him, she threw him to the ground and had her Fairbairn Sykes commando knife across his neck before she realized it was Smithfield.

"Bloody hell!" More afraid than angry, she said, "I could've killed you, fuckin' prick!"

While rolling on the ground, Smithfield said, "Bollocks! My fault, my fault. My God, Masters, you're bloody dangerous! I'm glad you're on my side."

She replied flatly, "Yes. Yes, you are. You're relieved, by the way."

She disappeared into the jungle.

Phillipe kissed Jenn goodbye and told her to meet him right after graduation so they could head to Vegas. He leaped to the front porch, but before he could open the door, Mary Rainbird had beat him to it.

"Where in the hell you been?" she said. This was a rhetorical question because she didn't wait for an answer and just continued. "Don't fix your mouth to lie to me. I saw you and that white girl in the van."

She didn't stop. "At least you could've invited her up for breakfast to say hello!"

By this time, Phillipe was preparing to get into the shower, but all the while, Mama hadn't broken stride.

"Damn, boy. You smell like funk plus function. I swear to God, if you make us late for your graduation and embarrassed this family . . . ooooh!"

Phillipe was nodding and whispering, "Yes, ma'am" as he closed the bathroom door.

June twelfth, 11:00 a.m. Sophie was awakening from her drug-induced stupor. Her eyes were barely focused when she glanced at her clock radio. She could feel the Los Angeles June gloom, a heavy overcast along the beach cities. This created very cool mornings, but once the dew point rose, the clouds burned off and the weather returned to seventy-five and not a cloud in the sky.

The window in Sophie's room was open, and a cool ocean breeze entered. She went to the bathroom first and sat down to pee. She could hear her television playing *The Price Is Right*, but there was a smell in the air. She tried to pinpoint whether it was from outside or inside. She finished peeing, wiped, and flushed the toilet, then walked slowly to track the smell. Suddenly, she recognized the smell as gas, and her first instinct was to call out to Bear, but there was no answer. Feeling something was wrong, she ran downstairs. In her haste, she hit the trip wire, and the pin pulled out.

Sophie saw the device before she could scream. There was a blinding light, and the entire house ignited into a fireball. In seconds, the wooden house was in flames. The cops outside, drinking coffee and talking, got hit by flying debris. The two adjacent houses caught on fire, and the police called for the fire department and backup.

The fire was a disaster. Three companies took two hours to put it out. There were two casualties—Bear and Sophie—and the DA's office wanted somebody's ass. Whether it was Big and/or the police, they didn't care. Hundreds of thousands of taxpayer dollars had been lost.

Detective Sergeant Adam Canaby, who was on scene, thought to himself, "Jeez, what a cluster fuck." He was in LAPD robbery/homicide and was a veteran cop of twenty years who'd had an encounter or two with the Strong family, particularly Bear. About ten years ago, when Bear was still street collecting, a pimp named Shakey had owed money to Bear for some numbers he'd played. Allegedly, Shakey owned an auto body shop as a front. Bear confronted Shakey, and a fight ensued, with Bear bashing Shakey in the head with a ball peen hammer. Canaby was personally involved because Shakey was his snitch. He investigated, but no witnesses came forward. Shakey's brand-new Cadillac was gone, never to be seen again. Ironically, Canaby was now in charge of Bear's murder investigation, and this made him chuckle. He was briefed by the arson investigator and told the obvious, but it was standard operating procedure, or SOP, to hear the fire experts go on about white phosphorus. Canaby bottom-lined the situation to one word: murder.

High school graduation—*boring*! Phillipe was nodding off during the self-serving speeches about the future and college. Blah blah blah. Phillipe had made more money last night than most people made in a six months.

After graduation, Phillipe got a chance to spend

time with the family before he and Jenn went to Vegas. He received a lot of very nice presents and cards with money. Jenn received a good (but funny) Christian lecturing from his grandma about premarital sex. The whole family knew that this was last time they would see Phillipe because he wasn't coming back before Monday morning. Phillipe had to report to the MEPS station at 5:00 a.m. on Monday, the sixteenth of June, and he was not going to let his parents drive him. Phillipe's Navy recruiter had told him to never let your mom drop you off at the MEPS because you look like you're in kindergarten. So, Phillipe and Jenn said their good-byes, and they got into the VW bus and sped away.

Danny Landon, the oldest of the twins by six minutes, played a slot machine while he watched Big from a distance— which wasn't easy. The MGM Grand's enormous size was striking, and since this was the start of the high tourism season, the casino was packed even at noon. Big was engaged in a high-stakes poker game of convenience, though he was a great player. Casinos are the best places to be seen. Lots of cameras, security, and witnesses. If something happened, like what Big had seen on the news this morning about a Venice Beach explosion, he was playing poker. Las Vegas police department's number one priority was the safety and security of the casinos, though that's not to say that if another police department or other law enforcement agency had a warrant, they would not honor it. But it was obvious where their bread was buttered. They wouldn't assist in harassment of paying customers because of some fishing expedition.

Phillipe had met the Landon brothers in 1975 at an Avon cosmetics party that Mary Rainbird was giving at her house. It was just after their father's funeral, and Mary was trying to support their mother, Anita Landon. Pat was so busy being a tour guide, she didn't realize that these two niggas were casing house. They kept asking questions like "When do y'all come and go" and looking to see how locks worked. So, based on the information Pat gave them, Phillipe knew they would show up some weekday when everyone was gone all day. He ditched school on Monday, and sure enough, he heard the doorbell ring a couple of times. A few moments later, he heard whispering, and the window of his room opened up. Danny stuck his head in, and there was a smile on his face until he saw the barrel of a 20-gauge shotgun pointed at his head. Phillipe invited big Dan for a little chat, and Sammy had to go sit in the car or he would blow his brother's face off. Basically, the conversation was a business proposition: Phillipe would give them jobs and all details needed for completion, and he would take 10 percent. Or Phillipe would tell Mama what he was doing, which was worse than calling the police. Danny could not have agreed faster.

The younger Landon, Sammy, was sitting in the eating area having lunch and watching Big and his girlfriend of the day. He did not recognize her. Big had a lot of women stashed, or maybe he had just met her. The important thing was that Sammy didn't see any of the family, and that made him uncomfortable. The family stuck together. If Big was there, they were probably in the neighborhood, and that meant they were hiding. "Maybe Phillipe was right," Sammy thought. "Big is going to try to save some money. Punk muthafucka!"

June twelfth, 8:45 p.m. The six-and-a-half-hour ride to Las Vegas was somewhat typical—lots of traffic through the counties of Los Angeles and San Bernardino. Depending on the time of day and traffic conditions, it could take two to three hours just to get to Victorville, which was only ninety miles northeast of the city of Los Angeles. And of course, there was the daily accident, usually involving a gasoline truck being hit by a match truck. Phillipe and Jenn were just happy to make it through the gauntlet. They rode through the middle-class neighborhood of Spring Valley, just a few miles west of the airport. In case everything went bad, they could get the fuck out of Dodge. Jenn wheeled the bus into the driveway of a medium-sized home, peach in color with a manicured lawn.

The crew had been able to buy real estate across the West Coast, with stolen money washed through a Nevada corporation. "Invest in your business," Big always said. These houses were great investments and staging areas, nothing to trace back. Big knew a Panamanian lawyer, and for 20 percent, the money came back clean. Nevada corporations were notoriously private for obvious reasons. Gambling was a multibillion-dollar business, and certain "organizations" were not going to walk away from it. Phillipe opened the front door with his key. The cool breeze flowed from the house, which was good news. The Nevada heat took some time to get used to, even at night. Phillipe looked through the house cautiously. He had his shotgun with a blanket concealing it. Jenn started to bring the bags in. Once Phillipe finished checking the house, he helped. The house was decorated with cheap but functional furniture. A cleaning service would show up two times a month or when needed. There wasn't any food in refrigerator, so Jenn suggested they go shopping now, while the temperature was under a hundred degrees. Phillipe thought, "Good point. Besides, I got to make a phone call."

The crime scene was a forensic evidence collection nightmare. If the fire hadn't destroyed it, the water had. The fire department's number one priority was not evidence preservation; it was saving lives and property. What Canaby did know was that this was murder. The arson investigators had found a military-grade phosphorus grenade, and the gas coupling to the stove had been taken off. The rescue team found two bodies, badly burnt, especially the female. She had caught it in the face. Hopefully, they could get dental records. Bear seemed to have a thin incision across the neck. To sum it all up, it was a professional hit, clean and organized.

Canaby thought, "Out-of-towners?" But how did they get in? Maybe the cops assigned to babysit had fallen asleep? Internal affairs was all over that. The chief of police and the mayor were involved, so there wasn't going to be any blue shield for those poor bastards. The only blind spot was the back of the house. When it was safe, Canaby took a long look in the large backyard where the doberman gang had been showing their displeasure at all the unwanted activity. Canaby felt something was off. The owners hadn't come to see why the dogs were making so much noise, and the house was dark.

A uniformed police officer passed by. It was Sergeant Kostel, who was in charge of the neighborhood canvas.

"Kostel!" Canaby yelled. "Did your guys check that house?"

Kostel said, "Yeah, we did. No answer at the door, though."

Canaby continued. "What about the neighbors? Have they seen those people?"

"Really didn't ask. We're more worried about the fire and getting the area sealed off," Kostel said.

Canaby went on his gut feeling that had served him well and said, "Sergeant, I need two uniforms and a paramedic team ASAP!"

June twelfth, 11:30 p.m. Phillipe was in a phone booth outside of a Safeway grocery store. Jenn was busy shopping and having fun. He waited a few seconds more, then dialed the number to another phone booth, predetermined by Phillipe. The phone rang four times before a woman answered. "Hello."

Phillipe said, "Are ready to shake your pants?"

The unidentified woman said, "You know it, suga', because I like the way you dance!"

Phillipe proceeded to give her instructions on how to make the drop. When he was finished, he asked her if she had any issues. Her reply was no, and Phillipe abruptly hung up. The woman who was in front of a 7–Eleven store hung up the phone and got back into her rental car and drove away. Across the street, Danny Landon sat in his car making sure that everything was OK.

After Canaby and Kostel debated the feasibility of anyone getting in the backyard with the dobermans and surviving, they both decided it couldn't hurt to check it out. The oak front door was going to be a bitch to breach. The paramedics thought it best to break open a window first. When they found the married couple in the bathtub, everyone was relieved. The rescuers worst fears were lifted. The Douglases were understandably scared and very soiled. After a shower or two, they were checked out by the paramedics. The officers made coffee, and Mr. Douglas fed and watered the dogs, which surprisingly shut them up.

Mrs. Ruth Douglas sat in the kitchen, contemplating the last twenty-four hours. She was embarrassed because she had evacuated on herself and a bunch of strangers had found her helpless in soiled clothes. Canaby reassured Mr. and Mrs. Douglas that they should be happy to be alive. The pair gave the same account—one large man wearing a ski mask and gloves and dressed in all black had appeared from nowhere, no noise to indicate where he came from. He had forced them upstairs into the bathroom. Mrs. Douglas said he was very polite. Even when he told them to empty their pockets, it was "Yes, ma'am" and "No, ma'am."

Canaby normally would have thought she was full of shit, but on the kitchen table were all their possessions. Nothing was missing from the house, and after an hour or so, they had both heard footsteps going down the stairs and the front door opening and closing. They didn't understand anything until the explosion.

Canaby asked one final question. "Did the you hear the dogs barking?"

Looking puzzled, they glanced at each other and both simultaneously said, "No!"

June thirteenth, 12:00 p.m., Las Vegas, Nevada. Caesars

Palace was by far the most opulent casino on the strip. The driveway leading up to the concierge was half a mile long. When a taxicab pulled up, someone immediately opened the door for the beautiful blonde lady. Jenn was dressed in a very chic white business pantsuit with matching hat and wearing dark sunglasses. As she walked by, she tipped the nice gentleman twenty bucks while smiling and said, "Thank you." She was carrying a Neiman Marcus shopping bag, and she walked with grace and purpose. She made her way to the slot machine area and sat down at a dollar machine.

A few minutes later, a black lady sat down next to her. The black lady was Big's girlfriend. She also had a Neiman Marcus bag. Jenn could see a garment on top but nothing else. Jenn glanced around and saw Sammy Landon. He gave the OK sign, so she pulled the arm a few more times. Jenn leaned in quickly to check out the contents of the bag. She saw hundred-dollar bills. She picked up the bag, turned, and said, "Good luck." The girlfriend replied, "You to."

Jenn walked out the same way she had come in. In no hurry, she told the concierge she needed a cab. He remembered that she was a good tipper, so he went to work. When the cab pulled to a stop, he opened the door. She tipped him and slid in gracefully. Once inside the cab, she told the driver, "Las Vegas Sands."

She did a thorough inspection of the contents of the bag, and everything seemed all right. She checked to see if she was being followed, but she saw nothing. The driver turned into the Sands driveway, and she repeated the same behavior when greeted by the concierge. But this time, she went straight to the elevators. The doors were already open, so she walked in and pressed the button for the seventh floor. Before the doors closed, she gave a quick glance to make sure that no one was there. The elevator stopped at the seventh floor, the doors opened, and she went swiftly to room 707.

Click. Jenn felt a knife against her ribs, and a male voice said, "Not a sound, bitch. Is your boyfriend in there?"

Jenn nodded yes, and the man continued. "Open the door slowly."

She complied, and they walked in. The room was a suite, decorated in classic Vegas opulence and decadent at the same time. They both moved in rhythm. The man heard the shower, and he whispered, "Call him out here now."

Jenn reluctantly said, "Hey, baby. I'm back."

Phillipe called out, "Hey, how did it go?"

She said, "About what you expected."

The man didn't like the last comment and started to threaten Jenn when he felt something pressed against his head.

He turned to find the biggest Indian he had ever seen holding a .22 caliber suppressed Ruger pistol. Apache Jack politely said, "Sir, please put the knife down, or I'll kill you."

Clearly intimidated, the man dropped the knife before Jack stopped talking. Phillipe appeared, and Jenn walked over to him. When the man turned to see Phillipe, Jack whistled and knocked him the fuck out.

Apache Jack was born in the summer of 1958. His given name was Jacob, and he had no last name. He had been left on the doorstep of a Catholic church with a note saying only JACOB. The monsignor saw that the child was an Indian. He knew Phillipe's grandfather Goya from a fellowship picnic and asked him to take the child. Both men knew that a child's chances of adoption in Mississippi were terrible. Goya said yes and raised the boy in the ways of the Chiricahua.

When Phillipe first met Jack, he thought he was the coolest cat ever because he never said very much and knew everything, or so it seemed. Jack showed Phillipe around the farm, and he answered all of Phillipe's dumb questions. The summer before Jack went to Pearl River Community College, Goya and Jack were tracking three escaped prisoners from Angola prison. Phillipe was there only to watch and learn. Allegedly, the escapees had armed themselves with a couple of shotguns and an axe they had stolen from a farm in Louisiana before they crossed the river into Mississippi.

Goya and Jack came through the dense foliage gracefully, making very little sound, stopping only occasionally for reassessment and communication. Goya would look at Jack, motion with his hands, and Jack would move without hesitation. Goya would look at Phillipe and say, "Stay close." Then Goya would defy the fact he was over seventy and sprint away at incredible speed, Phillipe struggling to keep up. Phillipe predictably got lost until he heard gunfire. He ran toward it, and near a clearing, he made himself small. Phillipe saw that prisoner number one was shot in the chest, and number two was yelling for a doctor. Goya has trying to talk number two down and find the location of number three. It was chaotic. Goya and Jack had moved so fast they were miles in front of the main force.

Phillipe saw a shadow. It was Jack coming into position behind number two. Suddenly, there was a smell of sweat, and a twig broke. Phillipe spun around. There was number three with a shotgun in hand aiming for Jack. All Phillipe had was a tomahawk that Jack had made for him. Pulling the tomahawk from his belt, he screamed, "Jack!"

Diving and rolling to get into a better position to cover/shoot, Jack pointed his shotgun in the general area of the shouting. Goya knew instantly who that was, so he opened fire on number two, killing him. Goya ran to his grandson's location. There he saw Phillipe standing over the body of number three. The man has bleeding from the side of his head, because there was a tomahawk buried in it. After checking the other two, Jack came over and said, "Thanks."

Goya put his arm around Phillipe. "You made me and your ancestors proud. You are now a Chiricahua. Just don't tell your mama. She will scalp me."

Phillipe looking confused and said, "Are you scared of Mama?"

Goya simply said, "Isn't everybody?"

Before Phillipe went back to LA, Jack asked if they could be blood brothers. Phillipe asked Jack if he could call him Uncle Jack, and Jack replied, "I will always be there for you. Just call me. But if you ever call me uncle, I'll kill ya."

June fifteenth, 9:00 a.m. Big was in his luxury suite at the MGM Grand. There wasn't any word from his guy. Big didn't know the guy's name and didn't want to. The word on the street was that he was very reliable, and Big wanted to keep his distance, especially since the guy's job was kill to Little. But, business is business, and Big wasn't getting the gas chamber for nobody.

A knock came at the door. Big thought it was room service with breakfast. A deep male voice said, "Police! Open up, please!" So, Big obliged. The police came in with hotel security and asked, "Are you Tracy Leonard Strong from Los Angeles?"

Big was so accustomed to this shit, he answered with no emotion. "Yeah. Girlfriend. Shower. No weapons or drugs. Lawyer."

Big's girlfriend appeared. The police asked her for identification, which indicated her name was Vilma Newhope, same name on the register. The police did a quick search and found nothing, so they went into cop mode Q&A. They threw Big all the obvious questions, and Big gave them all vague or standard "I don't know" answers. When the cops got frustrated, they made accusations that they could never prove, because they were looking for a prescribed response. Big, who was a veteran of police interrogation and had the Miranda warning memorized, kept his cool while politely requesting a lawyer again. The cops came with nothing and left with even less.

Moments later, Big was trying to get his head around some things. How did the Las Vegas police department know he was there? The room wasn't registered in his name, and he hadn't told anyone he was at MGM.

The knocking on the door interrupted Big's thought process. "Don't tell me these fools came back." He abruptly opened the door to find the room service attendant with a continental breakfast. Big relaxed and invited him in, remembering that he was hungry. Vilma signed, Big gave him a tip, and before the attendant left, he said he had a package for Mr. Strong. Big became paranoid, instructing him to put the package on the bar and demanding to know who had given it to him.

The attendant set down the box, which was wrapped like a present. Conveniently forgetting the twenty-dollar tip, he said a small boy had given it to him as a surprise for his daddy. Big told the attendant to leave, then carefully opened the present and revealed a two-way radio. The radio broke the room's silence with a familiar voice.

"Hey, Big. You got your ears on good buddy!"

Big knew it was Phillipe. He came back with, "Hey, Little. Where you at?"

Little said, "Closer than you think."

"I see," Big said. "So you coming by?"

"No, you're too hot," Little replied.

"You sent them here?"

"Yes. Would you like to call a truce?"

"Not sure I can," Big said. "The ball is rolling."

"Oh, you mean that Dracula-looking muthafucka you sent. Don't worry. I got him."

"What do you mean?" Big asked.

"He's alive, but I'm keeping him."

"Why?"

"Leverage against you," Little said.

"You threatening me, little nigga?"

"Yes. You either forget about this shit or I take Dracula to the Crowbar and tell him a story that his daughter will back up."

Big was so embarrassingly proud, he couldn't believe it. He'd been outclassed by a fuckin' eighteen-year-old.

Little finally said, "You there?"

"Yeah. OK, you got my word it's dropped. By the way, good luck in the Navy. Come by and visit sometime."

"You know that," Little said.

"What should I do with the radio?" Big asked.

Jenn said, "Shove it up your ass."

August twenty-fifth, 3:47 a.m., Herefort, Great Britain. Day three of SERE school, or Survival, Evade, Recover, and Escape—an evolution that measured one's breaking point. No weapons, food, or water was provided, no access to medical care if needed, and no help. Basically, a candidate was turned into a wild animal and hunted. If captured, the price was quite literally brutal, but everyone got caught or turned themselves in after four days, absolutely fatigued. Jungle training had taken its toll, and Helen's joints ached. She knew that she wasn't supposed to get caught, but maybe being tied to a chair was not the worst idea. At least she'd be sitting down.

She heard a rustling of footsteps and moved as fast as she could deep into the tree line. Crouching low, she tried to catch her breath. She peeked around the tree when she heard another rustling. She turned quick to see a rifle butt strike across her face.

August twenty-sixth, 5:30 a.m., Great Lakes, Illinois, United States. The Navy boot camp is the second easiest to pass the first being the Air Force—ten weeks of cleaning, marching, and yelling. Of course, in between all that, Ricky recruits learned basic firefighting/damage control, seamanship, and team building. After the first three to four weeks, the Recruits In Competition, or RICs, are on automatic. They know what to do and when to do it. Two weeks before graduation, the company commanders throttled down because they realized that if you ain't got it by now, you never will. Yelling and screaming was a waste of their time. The morning routine was normal—make up your bunk, wash up, get dressed, and get breakfast. Daily activities were moment to moment, and things changed quickly. Phillipe was a squad leader, which meant he had seven men to supervise, but no real authority. That was basically whoever the guys listened to.

Today was detailer day. A detailer was a person who wrote orders for naval personnel. The what, where, and when of a sailor's career was in the hands of a few unseen people. Phillipe and company were going to make sure that the detailer didn't fuck up their orders, which happened by accident and on purpose far too much. The entire graduation class, three hundred sailors, stood in one spot stood outside the detailer building for hours. What could possibly go wrong? By the time everyone was finished, it was dinnertime. Phillipe thought to himself, "Muthafuck me. Let's go." He was in the process of organizing his guys when his CC came over and screamed, "When I call your name, you are to report to room 212, second floor of this building. Anyone that doesn't report, I will fuck you up. Understood?"

The entire company yelled in unison, "Aye aye, sir!"

The CC called several names. The last one was

Rainbird.

Helen Masters awoke when she felt her clothes being ripped off. She struggled fiercely, but her hands were tied. She had been though SERE training before, and this wasn't the same. A feeling of helpless crept into her mind. This enraged her. If a wild animal was what they wanted, she would give them a show.

They picked her up and carried her to the interrogation room. They put her in a wooden chair. Her hands and feet were bound, and all she could think about has getting her hands on one of these fucks. Naturally, they all were wearing ski masks so no one could be identified after the gangbang. Cowards.

Helen looked around and said, "Excuse me. I was looking for a real man. Have you seen one?"

Masked man number one walked up and slapped her across the face saying, "Let me be first to welcome ya to the party. Now as I'm your host, it's not polite to offend me!"

"Fuck off!" was her reply.

Next, masked man number two punched her so hard that the chair flew across the room and burst into pieces. Helen was bleeding from her head and nose, and her right eye was swelling. The masked men in the room were yelling and cursing at each other. Masked man number one told number two to make sure she wasn't dead.

When he kneeled down to check Helen's vitals, she used her free hand to grab and twist his genitals. Her homicidal rage didn't stop there. She wrapped the other arm around his neck and pulled his nose into her mouth. She bit and would not let go. It was anarchy. The only way to get Helen to stop was for a rifle to butt her. Number two passed out from the pain, and all the masked men knew that the sergeant major was going to have someone's arse.

By the time Phillipe and the rest who'd been chosen had settled in, the rumors were flying. Like, are we getting kicked out? But Phillipe was contemplating why they were there. If boot camp did nothing else, it made you question yourself. At that moment, the class door opened, and three familiar people walked in—one tall, the other two short.

Phillipe remembered where he had seen these three before. It was during the water competency test, when all naval personnel had to show the ability to survive in the water for five minutes. Having this skill set was obviously important, but Phillipe was shocked at how many people joined the Navy who didn't know how to swim.

The tall one was in charge. Walking around, he said, "All right, sit down and shut the fuck up. The quicker we do this, the quicker we get out of here! I'm Senior Chief Crown. I shall read a brief statement from the Chief of Naval Operations: By order of the President of the United States, in accordance with the Holloway Commission, I authorized the Naval Special Warfare Command to conduct a trial fast track of no less than six months. All units and commands are hereby ordered to comply immediately with all requests for transfer to NSWC.

Needless to say, every RIC in the room had a blank dumb-fuck look on his face. Senior Chief Crown explained that the Holloway Commission had investigated the events of the failed attempt to rescue the hostages in Iran. The report was scathing to everyone—the White House, the Department of Defense, and the CIA. But no entity was called out more than the Navy, and their accountability included but wasn't limited to lack of responsibility in maintenance control, no interoperability with other branches of the military, and the inability to conduct special operations in non-permissible environments.

That last reason, Senior Chief indicated, was why their sorry asses were here. By 1980, Naval Special Warfare was allowed to wither on the vine, a bureaucratic term, since Vietnam, for what's in it for me. Senior Chief was visibly angry just talking about this. Phillipe thought, "That's fucked up, being called out by the bosses for a problem they created."

Senior Chief continued. "Basically, gentlemen, this a recruiting event for the Navy SEALs. We have a videotape to watch and a Q&A session. Do not leave before the video is finished. Afterwards, if you are not interested in signing the sheet, muster out and march to chow. Any questions? Good."

September fifth, 7:00 a.m. Helen Masters was packing her belongings, along with the few people who had completed selection. Twelve candidates out of the 200 who started, 94 percent attrition. There was no "graduation" from selection. One just survived and moved on to the next evolution of training. All SAS operators lived with not just the reality of death but also the possibility of being Returned To Unit or RTU'd.

Helen's interrogation ordeal was sobering. The

fallout was extensive. In Command Sergeant Major Morris Winston's report, he took full responsibility for the behavior of his men, but condemned their actions as unacceptable by SAS standards. The report afforded no apologies, but cleared Lieutenant Helen Masters of any wrongdoing. That was as complimentary as Sergeant Major would ever be. The bad news was that two of the four men were RTU'd. A third was put on probation pending command approval, which meant a desk job and a maybe they'll let you back in. The DS whose nose had been bitten off and whose testicles had been crushed, received a medical discharge.

Helen's face had healed, and she felt good. She wasn't moving away to just another barracks. She was getting an opportunity to serve in an actual unit on probation, or as a probee, six months of taking shite. She couldn't wait!

September fifth, 10:00 a.m., downtown Los Angeles. Detective Canaby was smoking a cigarette and reading the *LA Times*. Another headline: "Gas House Murder Investigation Stalled." He thought, "Who the fuck makes up this shit?"

Canaby sat in the hallway of the Los Angeles Police Department headquarters waiting to be summoned into the chief of police's office. The last time Canaby had been there was for an Internal Affairs investigation. His partner at the time claimed that a teenage suspect had a gun. Canaby never saw a gun and said so, but his partner said there were eyewitnesses. The chief was pressuring his captains to clean the mess up, and shit rolled downhill to Canaby to back his partner's story. Canaby knew his partner kept a cold piece, or untraceable firearm, so he lied about it. He magically got promoted, and his partner retired with a full pension. The mother of the kid, well, she got to plan a funeral and bury her son. This stuck in Canaby's craw. He couldn't let the guilt go. IAD retaliation was to spread the word on the street that he could be bought.

The chief's secretary told Canaby they were ready to see him. When he entered the room, he felt the eyes staring. He sat down, knowing it was meant to be an uncomfortable ritual. Since no else spoke, Canaby took the initiative. "Good Morning."

A few returned the courtesy, others mumbled, and the chief said nothing. The chief started the meeting by saying, "Thank you for coming. Please give your progress report."

Canaby ignored the first part of the statement, which suggested he wasn't ordered to be there. He looked around the room. It was a who's who of Los Angeles political hierarchy.

Canaby said, "As of today, we have no new leads on the so-called gas house murders."

"What seems to be the problem?" the chief asked.

"A lack of reliable witnesses and evidence, sir."

Politician one spoke up. "LAPD is showing a lack of responsibility."

"That's uncalled for," the chief replied.

"The chief is right," politician two said. "Blame should rest at the feet of those animals. What they did to that girl is disgraceful!"

Politician one said, "Animals? So the death of a white girl is more important than a black man?"

Politician two: "In this case, you damn right!"

The chief: "This is not productive. Detective, please continue."

Canaby: "As I was saying, we are working this case from all angles in conjunction with the FBI. This obviously was professional a hit. There aren't many guys that function at that level, but we will find them."

The chief thanked everyone for their input and assured them that these crimes would be punished. "Everybody's gone to their separate corners," Canaby thought, because he hadn't a fuckin' clue what to do next.

February third, 1981, 6:00 p.m., Los Angeles. Phillipe had never felt this excited. He had graduated from boot camp and SeaBee school within the last six months. He had excelled, but his next challenge was the infamous Basic Underwater Demolition/SEAL school, or BUD/S. Even though he had been awake since 4:30 a.m., his adrenaline was cranked up. Back at boot camp, when Senior Chief had said, "All those not interested in the fast track program, sign and leave," half of the guys had left.

Once they'd left, Senior Chief looked at everyone and said, "What a bunch of dumb asses." Everybody started to laugh, and he told them that this program should have been installed fifteen years ago, and that's why they were so far behind the British. He was right. One week after Eagle Claw, SAS executed a daring hostage rescue at the Iranian Embassy. Phillipe remembered reading about it and seeing it on TV. Senior Chief answered all the questions thrown his way, especially "Why us?" But Phillipe knew the answer for himself. He was a qualified junior lifeguard. After they all signed up, he offered his assistance in passing the Physical Fitness Test with extra pool training. Phillipe was hooked.

Being stationed in Gulfport, Mississippi, with five and a half months to go to SeaBee training, was great. Phillipe got to spend the holidays with the relatives, and that made Granddad very happy.

The SeaBees threw a big graduation party with lots of alcohol and women, just the way sailors liked it. Most of the guys had to wait for orders, but not Phillipe. He was going to Naval Special Warfare Command. He had less than a week to report, so he went home first to pick up his 1977 Volkswagen Super Beetle and to say hello to his family and friends.

The trip down to San Diego was relaxing, or maybe he was just happy to get out of Mama's house. Phillipe told his father exactly what he was doing, but with Mama he was a little vague. When Mary asked Phillipe about what kind of training he was taking, he would say diving or change the subject. Phillipe and his father both agreed to keep Mary in the dark for fear she would worry. The Rainbirds had family in San Diego—Peter Tudor, a distant cousin who was going to the University of California at San Diego.

One Phillipe's friends from boot camp, Augustus Petigrew, or "Grew," had volunteered for BUD/S and was already there. Grew was from Gary, Indiana, and he never wanted to go back. When he was offered NSW, he didn't think his wife would go for it. But when his wife, Jessica, heard that her husband had a chance to go San Diego, she started to pack. And she told him, "You do what you want. I'm going to California."

Phillipe suddenly realized he was hungry and hadn't eaten in over eighteen hours. He saw a sign along the 5 freeway that said Hideaway Cove Motor Inn. He thought, "Why not," got off at Del Mar Drive, and turned right for a few blocks.

Hideaway Cove had been an old surfer/biker bar since the fifties, and from the looks of it, no one had painted it since the fifties. But there was a full house, so maybe they had put the money into the cuisine.

When Phillipe entered the restaurant, it was like walking into a time machine—art deco tiling and fifties music. Phillipe's first thought was of *Happy Days*, but the aroma from the kitchen was nice, and everyone seemed to be enjoying themselves, so he sat at the counter.

A very cute brunette lady approached and said, "Welcome to the Hideaway. What can I get you?"

Phillipe replied, "Water and a menu, please."

The lady smiled and said OK. Phillipe noticed she wasn't dressed like the other waitresses. She returned with the water and menu, and he inspected both for cleanliness. Because, if a restaurant had dirty menus and water, the food would not be any better.

Observing this, the lady said, "That's smart not to trust a place you've never eaten at."

Phillipe said, "Nothing personal. Everything seems fine. What do you recommend?"

She glared and said, "Shrimp platter."

Phillipe agreed, but before she got too far, he said, "Tell your boss you're doing a great job." She turned and said, "I am the boss."

✳

February fourth, 1:00 a.m., Herefort. The dimly lit room was made even more so by all the cigar and cigarette smoke. The four men sat around reading newspapers and arguing politics. Next to them were mannequins. The room was a large—eighteen feet by twenty feet with a high ceiling. There was a closet and a window. The walls were a gray-slate color, with a rubber texture. This was the SAS kill house, a technically sophisticated shooting gallery for practicing Close Quarter Combat, or CQB. This, by far, was the hardest and most dangerous skill a probee had to learn. A live-fire exercise with live ammo that coordinated speed, aggression, and surprise. SAS. Shooting accurately while bullets were flying in a closed environment was the specialty of the SAS.

Helen Masters was point man on a four-man team. Smithfield was setting up a breach explosive on the door. The team could hear the casual banter inside the room. Some of it was pretty funny. The breacher signaled OK, and the rest of the team signaled OK individually. The team leader gave the countdown: execute, execute, execute. Then, BOOM! The shape charge blew the door open, and Helen was first through it, making a hard left around the doorjamb, or a buttonhook.

As she entered, she fired her HK MP5 in double-tap fashion with precise shots. Head shots only. She hit two targets before teammate two entered the room. Helen continued to the corner of the room. The whole team entered firing double taps at the targets, while the live hostages lay motionless. Helen stopped because this was her sector of responsibility. She turned quickly and fired another double tap. The gunfire stopped after five seconds.

The team leader yelled, "Clear," and the rest of the team yelled, "Clear." Sergeant Major Winston walked in and yelled, "All Clear." The assault team cleared their MP5s by uncocking the bolt and engaging the safety. All of the hostages returned to being upright, and the DS inspected the room for stray bullets and mannequins that weren't fatally wounded. Once the DS inspection was passed, the team leader yelled, "Debrief in the classroom in five." Helen thought to herself, "I really like this shite."

Once Phillipe had eaten, his youthful metabolism slowed down, and he began to think about Jenn. He knew she was dating, but so was he. She was one of his closest friends, and he was missing her. Lisa Carter was the proprietor of the Hideaway Cove Motor Inn. She had been a hippie protestor while at Berkeley, and she spotted Phillipe as a sailor right off. They talked about the difference between the sixties and the eighties, Reagan, and each other.

Phillipe had a few beers and talked until midnight. He realized it was too late to bunk at Grew's crib, so he asked Lisa if she had room. She said yes, so Phillipe told her thank you and made two phone calls. He called cousin Peter and Grew to let them know he wouldn't make it until tomorrow. He hung the phone up, and while he exited the restaurant, he looked for Lisa but did not see her.

He went to his Beetle, opened the trunk, and removed a medium-sized black bag. He heard footsteps approach from behind. It was Lisa. She held her hands up and said, "Here's the deal. These are the keys to your room. You can go up and get a good night's sleep. Or here's the key to my room. You won't get much sleep, but it'll be more fun."

Phillipe response was, "Well, let me see. Sleep or

kinky sex. Mmm. Sex!"

February fifth, 12:00 p.m., Inglewood, California. Donald Hendricks, or Birdman, was a typical two-time loser, institutionalized and stupid. He was a former Strong family member, emphasis on the word former. He'd gone independent and tried to rob a bank around the corner from where he lived. He reasoning for this caper was that the cops wouldn't believe anyone would do it so close to home. When Big heard this, he said, "That's the dumbest shit I ever heard. You do know that you're a known felon for armed robbery, and you're the first nigga they'll be coming for. Stupid muthafucka!"

Everyone had a good laugh, and no one took him seriously, but he wanted to prove them wrong. The day before the job, he went to the barbershop for a haircut and started bragging about what he was going to do. What he didn't know was that there was an off-duty police officer waiting for a haircut too. When he walked into the bank, the cops were waiting. He got busted, and Big was so pissed, he kicked Birdman out of the family. Birdman did seven years and was now out on parole, sitting across the street from a NIX check-cashing business.

Birdman and his three loser friends sat in a car down the street. Basically, the plan was that loser number one's ex-girlfriend worked for NIX. When she came to work, they would take her hostage and force the employees to open the security door. But when the ex appeared, number one was clumsy, stumbling of the car and yelling, "Hey, girl, wait up!"

All four losers awkwardly approached the ex, which

frightened her, and she ran into the NIX. They ran after her, and she screamed, "Help!" Losers two and three pulled out their guns and started shooting in the general vicinity, and NIX went on lock-down. Birdman dropped his gun and started running through the neighborhood. After a brief chase, he was caught.

Birdman knew his status. While riding to the Inglewood Police Department, he mentally searched for anything he might give the police to get off. He was in a full-blown panic, but then all of a sudden, he had it. He was so happy, he couldn't wait to say it. "I know who killed Bear!"

It was a beautiful, partly cloudy day with a cool offshore breeze. Phillipe knew it was time leave, but that didn't make it easier. He had finished cleaning up and packing. Lisa had eased his blues away. Before Phillipe left, she had fixed breakfast in the morning and lunch in afternoon. In between, they made each other feel good. They exchanged contact information and good-byes, and he was off to Coronado Island to check in.

The naval installation on Coronado was divided into two separate bases—surface warfare, or ships/aircraft, and amphibious, or special warfare. Crossing the high, arching Coronado Bridge for the first time could be staggering. "What a view," Phillipe thought. He had to get the car registered on base and sign in to his new command. That was the military paperwork, Phillipe thought. So, after four hours, he called up Grew and got directions to his apartment in Chula Vista. Driving to Chula Vista, he noticed that the neighborhood started to slowly look like Los Angeles. Chula Vista was a southern San Diego lower-middle-class community with lots of apartment buildings and liquor stores. It was a perfect place for military personnel and working-class folks. Phillipe found the address, which wasn't easy because all the apartment buildings looked alike. Much to Phillipe's surprise, Grew and Jessica were outside barbecuing steaks, dressed in shorts and tank tops. When Jessica saw Phillipe, she ran and hugged him. Grew shook his hand. They spent the rest of the evening eating, talking, and laughing. Good times.

Detective Sergeant Adam Canaby got a phone call from a Lieutenant James King. King knew Canaby from the academy, and they had worked on many cases together, even after King was transferred to Inglewood Police Department. King told Canaby that he had a possible lead on the gas house murders. Like most officers in the greater Los Angeles area, King felt the LAPD was being unfairly criticized. Due to political positioning and budgetary concerns, the police department was forced to work in two-man twelve-hour shifts.

The house in Venice Beach had been owned by a wealthy supporter of the mayor. When the house was destroyed, along with some adjacent homes, the insurance company wouldn't pay and left the city with a $2 million dollar tab. Normally, witness protection is handled by federal marshals, but because the Los Angeles District Attorney didn't want to share the credit, the feds walked away. LAPD requested an expenditure of at least ten officers and detectives, and also several houses in the area. The police chief and the mayor agreed that the cost was not warranted for the type of criminal they were dealing with.

Canaby parked in the designated visitor's spot and was

greeted by King. They exchanged professional courtesies.

"Hey, dickhead!" King said.

"Hey, shit for brains," Canaby replied. "I ways wondered why you liked to lick my face."

They shook hands and entered the building. While walking, they updated each other on all the events leading up to that point. There was a police officer guarding the door to the interrogation room, and Canaby thought, "At least they're taking it seriously."

When the door opened, the musty underarm smell invaded the nostrils of both detectives. After the water from their eyes cleared, there was Donald "Birdman" Hendricks.

Birdman was sitting in a chair sweating profusely, as if he was running a marathon. King gave the officer inside the room the nod to leave, and the officer quickly did so. Canaby sat down across from Birdman, and King walked around behind him.

Once the detectives had established control of the room, the conversation started.

Canaby: My name is Detective Canaby. I am the lead investigator on the gas house murders case. Lieutenant King tells me that you can me help. Now, before you open your mouth, remember, I can smell bullshit a mile away. And quite frankly, the way you smell, that might be an improvement. Now speak to me."

Birdman: "First, you gotta get me outta town. If Big finds out that I'm dropping a dime, my ass is dead!"

King: "Hey, shit bag. You're already dead. You're about to do twenty-five to life, and we will spread the word that you cooperated. Then you'll be really dead."

Canaby: "This is what I call being between a rock and hard dick. No good choices. But if you tell me something valuable, I will help you."

Birdman: "OK, I heard it was Little who did it."

King: "Who is Little?"

Birdman: "I don't remember names. He was just a little nigga runnin' around when I was in the family. Like a mascot and shit."

Canaby: "What makes you think he did it?"

Birdman: "That's the word, man."

Canaby: "OK, where can I find him?"

Birdman: "I don't know. Ask around the hood."

King: "So, somebody told you that someone named Little killed Bear? Asshole, you're going to jail!"

Birdman: "Nah. Cuz I'm serious!"

Canaby: "All right. How old is Little?"

Birdman: "Back then, he was ten or eleven. Check it. Bear whoped Lil's ass 'cause he was talkin' shit. The last time I heard, Lil was at the park, you know. Him and Bear were fightin', and he beat the fuck outta Bear. And then Lennox shot Bear. Y'all should memba that shit. C'mon, man. Cut me some slack."

Canaby and King both got up and walked out of the

room.

Phillipe's itinerary was consistent until the start of BUD/S. He was now in pre-indoctrination, or pre-indoc. The day was chockful of fun activities, starting at 0600 with physical fitness for four to six hours, then medical and dental examinations, psychological evaluations, and lots of paper work. Six days a week, for the next three weeks. After that it would get worse, but Phillipe put that in the back of his mind. He was going to be hanging out with cousin Pete.

The Tudor family was on Phillipe's maternal side of the tree. Most of them lived in Oakland, California. Peter had gotten a scholarship to play basketball, and he was starting as point guard at UCSD. Phillipe and Pete hooked up to go to a frat party thrown by the Alphas. Phillipe did not want to spend his day off sitting on the base. Being around some new faces would be fun.

Phillipe found a parking spot and allowed Pete lead. The party was loud and packed with people. The frat house was huge. Its construction was pre-World War II. Half of the house was being used for the party. The other half was a designated social area. Pete went to the party side to talk to someone. Phillipe stood in the middle trying to decide between party or social. He decided, when in doubt, choose women. The women sitting and socializing looked prettier, so he ventured forth.

The room was spacious, and there was a small buffet. Phillipe made eye contact with all seven ladies and smiled. He said, "Hello ladies," and the ladies simultaneously said, "Hello."

He walked over to the buffet, picked up a plate and fork. He was deciding what to eat when a very attractive black woman came over and said, "Can I help you?"

"I'm fine, thanks," Phillipe said.

They began talking. She introduced herself as Michele Matthews. The ladies in the room were chaperones, and the buffet was for them. Phillipe apologized for the intrusion, but kept right on eating and flirting with her. Apparently, Michele was a graduate student, just a few months away from her MBA. Phillipe told her that he was in the Navy, that he was new in town, and that he needed a tour guide. She was reluctant at first, but after few drinks and dances, she agreed.

Kids. That's what Detective Canaby kept saying to himself. Kids. When he and Lieutenant King left the room, they debated the weird possibility that kids pulled off the cleanest hit in history. King's position was that Birdman would say anything to save his ass, but Canaby was more pragmatic. He had to consider the possibility. Kids. While driving back to the LAPD headquarters, his mind was busy putting the pieces together. King had done the right thing. First, calling to give the heads-up. Most cops stay in their jurisdiction, and if another cop comes sniffing around, whole departments and agencies start having pissing contests. Second, even though King didn't believe a word of the story that Birdman had told, he still held sway as a material witness, just in case. Kids. There's that fuckin' word again, which makes no sense and perfect sense.

No sense—for Big to trust kids with a job this important. Sense—if Big did use kids, the police would waste time chasing the usual suspects for years. No sense—what kind of fuckin' kid could do it? Does he have a record?

Canaby's confusion didn't outweigh his fear of the thought that a kid could scout, plan, and execute a hit so vicious. Canaby thought of his own son, Albert, sixteen years old and a great kid. Albert was an average student, very popular, but quite frankly, Canaby couldn't trust the boy to take out the fuckin' garbage. Kids. Fuckin' kids. It made perfect sense! Kids!

Canaby remembered one of his favorite movies, *To Sir with Love*, with the scene where Sidney Poitier gets really mad at the behavior of his class. He leaves the classroom and goes to the teachers' lounge, and after a moment of reflection, he has an epiphany to change the teaching curriculum. He thinks inside of the box and finds the solution to the problem with one word. Kids!

San Diego, California, was a beautiful city of rich scenery and great weather. Unlike other cities that have a large military presence, San Diego felt more like a resort. Michele took Phillipe to the world-famous San Diego Zoo, and they strolled along casually, looking at animals being secondary to being together. The more Phillipe knew about her, the more he liked her.

Michele Matthews was the only child of Micah Matthews, a real estate and car dealership mogul. Mr. Matthews had been a marine in Korea, and had landed at Inchon and fought at the Battle of Chosin. A tough bastard, Phillipe thought. After the war, he had gotten transferred to Camp Pendleton in Oceanside, a little north of San Diego, and met his wife, Christine. He had built his company from scratch with no loans, working eighteen-hour days for years. Michele was being groomed to take over the empire, but she wanted to make it on her own. Phillipe was very impressed with her. Good looks are one thing, but brains and pride are a rarity.

They continued to walk and talk about everything. It was easy. There was chemistry between them. When they left the zoo, it was getting dark, and they both were hungry, so they went to a local family restaurant and continued their interaction. The conversation turned to the inevitable— should they or shouldn't they. They mutually decided yes.

Michele's apartment was in La Jolla, a very upscale neighborhood in northern San Diego. The next morning was special because they communicated verbally and nonverbally, no wasted energy on who is thinking this, that, or the other. Which was important because Michele was borderline nympho, and Phillipe knew he needed all his energy to hang in there. Phillipe promised to keep promises if Michele would be understanding of his situation. This made the atmosphere fun and inviting, things Phillipe could only hope for.

Chapter 5

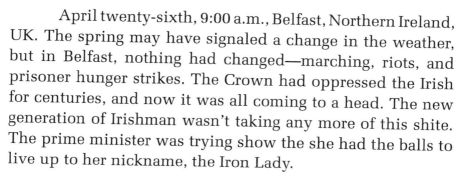

April twenty-sixth, 9:00 a.m., Belfast, Northern Ireland, UK. The spring may have signaled a change in the weather, but in Belfast, nothing had changed—marching, riots, and prisoner hunger strikes. The Crown had oppressed the Irish for centuries, and now it was all coming to a head. The new generation of Irishman wasn't taking any more of this shite. The prime minister was trying show the she had the balls to live up to her nickname, the Iron Lady.

"Bollocks!" Rafferty thought as he watched the ugly cunt on the telly. His anger was about to be unleashed upon this two-faced twat. She was dead and didn't know it. He looked around the flat and marveled at all the hard work he had put in. The old Sinn Féin leadership didn't have the balls to conceive of the assassination of the PM. The plan was a go. All he had to do was use the shortwave radio he had hidden in the flat. Then, ten attacks simultaneously across the UK. At the same time the PM would be giving a speech at an orphanage, the IRA would have its greatest victory. One shot to the head and done.

Jimmy Rafferty, third generation IRA, was a true hater of the British and wanted to remove their stench from his beautiful isle. He heard the all-too-familiar sound of his neighbors arguing. They had moved in next door a couple months ago, a bloke and his mum. Two pains in the arses, they were. And the two were at it again. Rafferty thought to himself, "These are the only two fucks on this whole fuckin' isle who ain't British that me wanna kill!"

A knock on the door snapped Rafferty into soldier mode. He whispered, "Who's there?"

"It's me, Karl. For fuck's sake, open the bloody door before I shite myself!"

Rafferty opened the door, and Carl ran by and said, "Me arse is on fire. Fuckin' move!"

Rafferty laughed at Karl O'Shea's dilemma. While the door was open, he saw the old woman and young man arguing. Trying to be respectful to Mrs. Shamus, Rafferty said, "Ma'am, could ya two keep it the fuck down. I fuckin' can't think straight!"

Mrs. Shamus turned with her hands on her hips and said, "Go shite in a bag and punch it!"

Mrs. Shamus and son went back into their flat, and Rafferty mumbled "Twat" under his breath. He went back inside to watch the telly. Karl finally came out, bringing the shite smell with him. Rafferty and Karl gave each other shit for a while until Rafferty motioned that it was time to start the operation.

All of a sudden, there was knock on the door and a loud argument outside. Rafferty, completely pissed, opened the door, and a small breaching charge went off. The door was blown off the hinges, and Rafferty went flying across the room, hitting his head on a table. Karl's vision was blurry, but he could make out two people. A man quickly approached with a machine gun. Karl froze with fear, putting his hands up.

When the smoke and his vision cleared, Rafferty saw Mrs. Shamus standing over him with a Browning Hi-Power 9mm fitted with a suppressor pointed at his head. Karl was being handcuffed. Mrs. Shamus jumped on his neck with her knee and spoke in a proper British accent, "We only need to arrest one of you. If you don't tell me where the others are, I'll kill you right now."

"OK! OK! Who the fuck are you?" Rafferty yelled.

Helen Masters commanded Rafferty to turn over and put his hands behind his back. Helen was a part of 14 Field Security and Intelligence Company, or The Det, the British Army's answer to the deficient intelligence apparatus concerning counterterrorism. The IRA seemed to be one step ahead of the British forces during the sixties and seventies, so when MI5/MI6 failed to give adequate intel, the Army decided to do it themselves.

When Helen returned to the farmhouse where The Det was headquartered, the entire British military and intelligence services were busy raiding all of Rafferty's known IRA safe houses in the UK. Helen walked in and was greeted cheerfully by the support staff. She headed directly to the locker room to change and remove the makeup. After a good, long hot shower, she entered the debrief room. Three gentlemen sat behind a large table eyeballing her.

She closed the door, took three steps, and said, "Lieutenant Masters, sir!"

Official one: "At ease, lieutenant. Give your report."

Helen: "Sir! My teammate and I posed as Belfast commons. I played the mother, and he played the son. Six weeks ago, we moved in next door to a suspected IRA communication hub. We pretended to argue loudly the entire time, to cover the noise of the drilling and annoy the terrorists, while we worked on putting a fiber-optic camera microphone in place. Our surveillance proved to be a wealth of information. We were able ascertain details of their plans. When we gathered enough intel and the threat was imminent, we acted straight away. We captured two terrorists, communications equipment, weapons, and documents. The two men are cooperating. Mr. Rafferty was the only casualty, with a severe concussion and multiple lacerations to the face. His prognosis is positive."

The three men looked at each other nodding, and official one said, "Well done, lieutenant. We hear you're taking a well-earned holiday. Outstanding! Dismissed."

Most American boys who play team sports have heard of something called hell week. Basically, it's a week-long series of multiple practices of two or three days to test your heart. BUD/S version of hell week tests something more precious—a man's spirit. Because, unlike sports where the individual goes home and gets some sleep, at BUD/S it's twenty-four-hour days with maybe three hours of sleep for the entire week. Sports can be dangerous in certain situations. BUD/S is dangerous all the time.

Phillipe was one hell of a baseball player and a damn good athlete, but his ass was dragging. He was learning that nothing truly prepared anyone for this. Even the first seven weeks of BUD/S was just a taste of this enormous shit. Phillipe put his mind on cruise control. He tried to focus only on what he was doing, which was hard. Between Michele, family, and friends, it was only natural during high-stress situations to think happy thoughts. Phillipe's mind was his greatest asset. It had served him well, but now it was his biggest weakness unless he could turn it off. He focused on his running and staying efficient, breathing deeply. Three miles down; three miles to go.

Early morning on a Monday, Detective Canaby was waiting outside in his car. He saw Mary Rainbird get into her car and drive toward the freeway to her job. He just wanted to see the mother of the devil, or Phillipe Rainbird, because the more he learned about this guy, the more Canaby believed that he was the one. The gas house killer.

Canaby had spent the last two months tracking this kid down, and what did he find? Nothing that he expected. The Rainbird family was a great bunch of people. No career felons, no institutionalized mentality, no foster home. No fuckin' reason that this kid should be a part of this shit.

Canaby had gotten Phillipe's school records and talked to some of him teachers. The kid could have gone to MIT, but with no scholarship money, he had gone into the Navy. Rainbird did have a sealed juvenile record. Otherwise, he was a parental dream. Canaby thought his son would be lucky to get into a junior college. Here was the hard part: How in the fuck did he convince anyone of this kid's guilt. He could barely believe it. Canaby thought for a moment, then decided to run it up the flagpole. So he went back to headquarters and set up a meeting with the bosses.

Once Canaby finished his speech on the theory of kids being the perpetrators in the gas house murders case, his bosses looked at him in a way that was both demeaning and infuriating. They wanted to know how long it had taken for him to come up with this bullshit. His lieutenant stood up and indicated that if the chief heard that shit, Canaby would be fired before he'd finished. After Canaby was thoroughly chastised, the discussion changed to whether not he was the right person for the job and maybe it was time for some fresh eyes. That's when he was assigned a rookie detective by the name of Barnes. Canaby knew that this was their way of saying: Get ready to retire or we will find something so we can fire you.

The train from London to Brighton was long but relaxing. Helen didn't get to see her Nana often, and they both were looking forward to it. The train pulled into the station, and she retrieved her bags and exited.

The station was crowded with people commuting back and forth to London. Helen hailed a cab. She gave instructions to the driver, and off they went. The cobblestone street felt familiar during the ride, as did the sights. The Brighton sea air smelled like home. The cab drove past St. Michael's Church. Helen thought of Father Reilly, a good man who had helped out when her mother died. They passed Helen's high school, Brighton and Hove, and she tried to remember the good times. But her accelerated academic curriculum had been so demanding, there was little time for fun. She had enjoyed beating the boys at futbol, not an endearing quality when climbing the adolescent social structure. Helen could see Nana's house and the ocean. The fog of the morning was burning off. Then she saw the police in front of the house.

May third, 2330, Coronado Island, San Diego. Phillipe's hobbled stance said it all. He wasn't sure what day it was or exactly what he was being asked to do. However, he had managed to overcome his weakness. His brain was offline.

Not only that, he wasn't following orders. Phillipe was on automatic. He was just following the rest of the guys, or at least what was left of class one three something or other. Phillipe's arms felt as if they were going to fall off because his seven-man boat crew had carried around a two-hundred-pound rubber fuckin' boat for a week straight. Not to mention the twenty-foot telephone poles. And between all that, five-mile open-ocean swims, a killer obstacle course, seven- to ten-mile runs, and class work, etc.

Standing without moving was becoming a task at the moment Master Chief Mayberry spoke, "Alrighty, this is your chance to do yourself and everyone else a fuckin' favor and quit! This shit will go on and on. You fuckers don't deserve to be on my fuckin' grinder! C'mon, I know there's a quitter somewhere."

Just then, a guy from another boat crew broke formation and walked across the grinder, or exercise area, to the quitter's bell to ring out. Ringing out is an embarrassing ritual a sailor must go through to announce that he is quitting training. Once the guy rang the bell three times, all the instructors clapped their hands and cheered. The trainee was led away for out-processing. The master chief looked at everybody and said, "Anyone else? Okay, suit yourself. Class leader!"

"Yes, Master Chief!" responded the class leader, or the highest-ranking trainee.

"I want every swinging dick to sing the theme from *Gilligan's Island* right fuckin' now!"

Since, all of the trainees were brain dead, they all started to sing in a confused and apprehensive matter: "Just sit right down to hear a tale, a tale of a fateful trip, that started from this tropic port aboard this tiny ship. The mate was a mighty sailing lad, the skipper brave and sure. Five passengers that day for a three-hour tour, a three-hour tour. The weather started getting rough. The tiny ship was tossed. If not for the courage of the crew, the passengers would be lost. The ship's aground on this uncharted desert isle, with Gilligan, the Skipper too, the millionaire and his wife, the movie star, the professor, and Mary Ann here on Gilligan's Island."

Of course, it took a couple of restarts, and even then, guys were mumbling the words they forgot or didn't know. Master Chief made the class stand there a few moments, waiting for the next evolution until they heard, "Secure from hell week, class leader! Muster at 1500 for inspection."

Phillipe's legs could barely move. It wasn't the muscles as much as the joints. He got halfway to his barracks and thought, "Inspection?" He couldn't drag all this sand and dirt into the barracks, which they had already cleaned before hell week. Everyone slept in tents on the beach. So he yelled to his fellow trainees not to go inside yet. "We're too dirty!"

The class stopped short of walking in. They realized Rainbird had a point. So everyone debated what to do. Then Phillipe got an idea. There was a firefighting station or equipment near the building, with several attachments and hoses. Phillipe connected the one-and-a-half-inch hose, and the other trainees got the gist. They spanned into areas to assist with the hose. The class leader attached the nozzle for the fire curtain. To protect the members of a fire team, another sprays water over them, using it like a huge outdoor shower. Phillipe and the class leader manned the hose while the rest of the class undressed and rinsed off. Some of the trainees collected dirty fatigues.

Phillipe was next. He peeled off his garments and stepped under the ice-cold water. His metabolism went into hyperdrive, and he was rejuvenated enough to walk to the barracks to get his keys. Butt naked and dripping wet, Phillipe walked to his car. Lieutenant Tolliver, the class leader, screamed "Rainbird! Where you goin'?" Phillipe didn't answer because he couldn't turn around. He only had enough strength to walk forward.

The lieutenant, feeling something was wrong, jogged awkwardly toward Phillipe. When the lieutenant caught up, he said, "Hey, man! What the fuck you doin'?"

Phillipe whispered, "I'm going home to take a bath."

"Dude, you know you're naked, right?" Tolliver said.

Phillipe replied, "I got some shoes in the car."

May fourth, 10:00 a.m., Carrighton General Hospital, Brighton, England. Helen sat impatiently in the visitor's lounge, a place that was all too familiar. It was the same hospital where Mum had passed on. The sickening feeling got worse, especially when a doctor walked back. She was wanting to know but not wanting to know.

Ida "Nana" Simon had suffered a stroke, to what extent no one knew. The cleaning lady had found her face down on the floor. It would seem that Nana was preparing breakfast while smoking, and had fallen and hit her head on a chair. The only good news was that her lit cigarette had landed underneath her and was extinguished. Otherwise, the house would have gone up in flames.

Now, dealing with the aftermath was the hard part.

Father Reilly was the first person to arrive. He was always there with a positive attitude, a true friend of the family. Clara, the cleaning lady, was visibly shaken while talking to the police. And then Helen saw a face she had not seen in years— Edward Whittingham, a man who had been Helen's first real crush. He was so dashing, and even in Helen's grief, she was smitten. He made eye contact, and her knees got wobbly. He walked over and gave her a warm embrace, apologizing for being late. Edward expressed his condolences and offered his assistance in any way. Helen's eyes were completely star struck. She smiled and said thank you, but refrained from saying anything else so as not to sound like an idiot.

Eventually, the doctor met with Helen privately to say that Nana had suffered a major stroke to the temporal lobe. Her speech and memory could be affected long term. Helen was so upset, she stared closely until a chair was found. Edward talked to the doctor about the next steps and what to prepare for. While sitting, Helen reminisced on how Nana had always been there for her. The burning questions in her mind were: What now? What shall I do?

Edward came over. Holding her hand, he said, "It'll be all right. We'll get through this together." That was all she could hope for.

Phillipe awakened in haste, not remembering how he had gotten to Michele's apartment. Did I dream of hell week? At that moment, Michele woke up and said, "You're up. Good. I was worried. Other than the fact that you were breathing, you seemed dead or in a coma."

"What day is it?" Phillipe snapped.

Looking puzzled, Michele said, "Sunday morning. You don't remember coming here naked?"

Phillipe felt the urge to take a shit. He jumped out of bed and ran to the bathroom, barely getting there in time.

Michele gingerly approached the bathroom door and heard violent gastric noises sounding like a war movie. She knocked and said softly," Babe, you need a doctor?"

Phillipe moaned, "I'm cool. I'll be all right. I'm angry."

Michele told him OK and walked into the kitchen and started breakfast.

Phillipe's face was in his hands when he started remembering the events of last night. Before Phillipe had gotten into his Beetle, he'd told the lieutenant that he'd be back at 1330 and sped away at a high rate of speed. When he'd gotten to Michele's apartment, he had forgotten two things. He didn't call first, and she lived on the second floor.

Phillipe's legs had been so tired that he could hardly work the clutch, so he found a parking space across the street. He'd stumbled to the security gate and prayed she'd let his nasty ass in. He pushed the button a couple of times. A weary voice answered, "Who is this?"

"Phillipe," he forced out. The gate buzzed, and Phillipe entered in a staggering fashion and began climbing the stairs. He got three steps from the top and collapsed. He crawled the rest of the way and knocked on the door.

Michele swung the door open so she could get with him for being disrespectful, only to find her man lying on her doorstep. She went from anger to panic. "What is wrong with you? Do you know you're naked? Are you drunk? You better not be!"

After hearing all that, Phillipe looked up and said, "Baby, could you please yell at me inside."

Once Phillipe got into the apartment and answered her questions, she realized what was going on. She also noticed the unusual stench coming from Phillipe and said," Get your ass in that tub first, and don't sit on my furniture!"

Phillipe soaked in the bathtub for an hour. He was so dirty, the water turned black. Michele laid out a sweat suit and made hot soup with a salad. The warmth of the water felt like heaven, and Phillipe drifted off to sleep. Michele had to wake him up before he drowned.

Phillipe got out of the tub, leaving a ring around it that looked like Daytona. After eating and drinking lots of water, he felt sleepy. Michele helped him into the bedroom, and he was asleep before he hit the mattress.

Once Phillipe's bowels stopped moving, he took a shower, and with a slow walk entered the kitchen, where he noticed the time was 7:45 a.m. He sat and ate breakfast. He shared his itinerary with Michele. After listening, she said flatly, "You owe me."

Phillipe knew he wasn't going to get much sleep.

September eighth, 4:17 a.m., Hollywood, California. Joseph Barnes had been on the Los Angeles police force for five years, after spending six years in the United States Army as a ranger. Because of his youthful appearance, he was assigned to narcotics and exceeded all expectations. For his many accomplishments, he rapidly was promoted to detective and assigned to homicide. His partner was Sergeant Canaby, who wasn't thrilled to wipe noses. Presently, the two were on a stakeout of a possible drug negotiation in Hollywood Hills. The parties involved were Big Trace Strong and a new player from New Orleans, whose name was not known at the moment. That information was still forthcoming. Canaby thought to himself, "No matter what, Big is going down one way or another."

Big was nervous about this meeting with Rufus Jackson, or Nahlense, which was the slang term in the black community for New Orleans. That was where Rufus Jackson was from, and he was the man at the port. So anything coming or going, a nigga had to business with Nahlense.

Big had heard of his reputation as a ruthless muthafucka and smart businessman. Rufus had cut the competition a new asshole, and Big was determined to let this country ass nigga know the deal. When the doorbell rang, Big Trace and the Strong family got into positions. Huey opened the door.

Huey was the new family enforcer since Bear had fallen off. He invited Rufus and his number-one boy, Sonny, into the apartment. Huey started to search them when Rufus politely indicated that he'd been searched downstairs.

Speedy, another longtime family member, yelled, "Nigga, this is upstairs! You got a problem!"

Rufus defused the situation by remaining under control and never raising his voice. "This dude is smooth," Big thought. Rufus was tall and lean, with a dark southern complexion. He had several gold teeth, and he was always smiling. He looked around at the view of the city. He extended his hand and introduced himself to Big, who did not pay Rufus the courtesy of standing. They shook hands quickly.

The conversation proceeded:

Big: "Sit down. Let's do this."

Nahlense: "OK. Excuse me for being so impressed. You LA niggas is livin' good than a muthafucka. I could get used to this shit."

Big: "Look, man. I need a reliable source. Is that you?"

Nahlense: "Yeah. My shit is tight like a virgin's ass."

Big: "Good. Because this shit here is big time, and you fuck up, it's yo ass!"

Nahlense: "Big, man. You doing me solid, man. Everybody know you, man. I'm just trying to ride yo coattail. I'm goin' make sure you get what you need, baby."

Big: "A'ight, we'll see."

Nahlense: "Befo I raise up, tell me, man, who'd you use to pop Bear? That was some cold shit. Can you hook a nigga up?"

Big: "Bye, nigga."

Nahlense and Sonny left the building, got into the car, and drove away. Sonny glanced at Nahlense, saying, "What you think?"

Nahlense, not smiling and thinking about what had just transpired, said, "I think I goin' to own this town, and all them niggas gotta go."

The last few months for Helen had been hard, seeing her Nana not being able to talk and all the hard work of rehabilitation. Nana was frustrated with the process and the changes in environment, not to mention that her personal habits had to change. Nana's world of independence was turned upside down, and Helen took an indefinite leave of absence. She had some serious soul searching to do. Besides, she was developing more than a friendly relationship with Edward. All the negative was offset by his presence. He was so chivalrous. He treated Helen like a queen, and she loved him and was beginning to think he felt the same way.

Nana was being cared for by the nurse, and Edward and Helen went for a bite to eat, a quiet night on the town and romantic conversation. The small eatery was cozy, the seafood excellent. All the patrons were people who lived in the area. French wine and candlelight, and the mood was set. Helen never thought much about her personal life. That was changing.

Edward said he had good news. He was moving back to London and suggested that Helen come with. Helen expressed her joy, but then remembered Nana's condition and the Service. Edward thought a twenty-four-hour nursing home would be appropriate. Helen scoffed at the idea of Nana locked up and resented the suggestion. Edward quickly backtracked, verbally maneuvering Helen to a positive subject of visitation with his family in Hyde Park. Helen let her guard down again, accepting his apology and invitation. Helen's mother had been the Whittingham's family physician, and Barbara Simon had held them in high esteem because the Whittinghams had referred her to all their friends. This gave her a chance to practice medicine privately and to mix in better social circles. And by extension, Helen could get into the best schools and marry a well-to-do man.

Helen and Edward walked to the front door of Edward's

flat. They knew that the time was right. Edward opened the door. The room was large and comfortable. Edward had impeccable taste in furniture and in the way he dressed. Helen's nervousness was apparent, and Edward sensed it, but he was nervous too. He reassured her with words that gave Helen confidence that everything was all right. She trusted his judgment and was finally caught up in the moment of passion.

San Clemente Island was the place where no one can hear you scream, or so Phillipe's instructors said. Master Chief mused that whatever happens happens. Phillipe and thirteen of his surviving classmates were entering the final exam of Land Warfare, a cumulative exercise of all that had been learned in BUD/S. Phillipe ran the operation, or op, though his mind: amphibious infiltration, topographic survey of the beach, clandestine approach and surveillance, identify location of POWs, extract, and aerial exfiltration. What could possibly go wrong?

Phillipe prepared himself for the water jump from the helicopter. Everyone took their predetermined places. At the go signal, they jumped one at a time. They swam in a formation of three teams. Gold team, an eight-man element, was headed by the class leader, Lieutenant Tolliver. Blue team, a four-man element, was headed by Jimbo, a first class petty officer. Red team, a four-man element, was headed by Phillipe, an E4. Gold team was flanked on the right by Red team and on the left by Blue team.

The underwater approach was flawless. Each team had mapped the shoreline in their sector. Once completed, the teams signaled good to go. Each team sent an advance scout to get eyes on. The scouts, if satisfied, gave the all clear, and the entire class walked to their respective areas and moved silently though the woods.

After a few kilometers or clicks, they came upon a small village. The class surveyed and took photographs. Suddenly, the class heard loud screams. Tolliver tried to give orders when the shooting started. The class was completely disoriented. Phillipe gave orders for his team to remain calm and fall back. The radio traffic was frightening, lots of yelling, The three other guys in Phillipe's team were debating whether they should go help the others. Phillipe calmly told them to be quiet and stay disciplined.

The Red team was ambushed from all sides. Since it was a live exercise, Phillipe threw three punches at somebody's face and ran through the foliage. It felt normal, just like Mississippi. Phillipe ran to a clearing and turned to see who was chasing him. He thought, "Oh shit, it's instructor Dietrich." Dietrich was a six-foot-five, 250-pound monster. His blue eyes pierced the darkness, and he was yelling like a wild animal. But Phillipe was much quicker. Dietrich was a bull blasting though everything in his path, disregarding thorny foliage, and his frustration increased with every step.

Phillipe barreled through a bush and came face-to-face with a giant spider with a gargantuan web. He leaned backwards and barely slid under it. Dietrich came bursting through but wasn't agile enough. Dietrich quite literally kissed the spider, which caused the spider and the web to wrap around him. Dietrich was on the ground yelling that the fuckin' spider was biting him. Phillipe didn't come close because he hated spiders, and giant spiders were at the top of the list. When the spider got tired of playing with its new friend, it wandered off. Dietrich had pissed in his pants.

After Phillipe flexible-cuffed the monster, he found a radio and a map with all the goodies, surveillance blind spots. The monster said he needed a medic, and Phillipe said, "I need to pass, muthafucka!"

Phillipe read the map and found an excellent spot. He could see the village, and the class was in cages. Phillipe wasn't pleased to see cages, but he saw no easy approach, so he needed the monster to make a deal. Phillipe could hear all the instructors' radio traffic, and they knew the monster was missing. The negotiations:

Phillipe: "Hello, is anybody out there? I'm just comfortably numb."

Master Chief: "No bullshitin' on the radio. Who is that, anyway?"

Phillipe: "Red team."

Master Chief: "Is that you, Rainbird?"

Phillipe: "Yeah. Let's make a trade."

Master Chief: "Why would I do that?"

Phillipe: "Because your boy is dying. He got bit in the face by a giant spider."

Master Chief: "Is he conscious?"

Phillipe: "Yeah, talk to him."

Phillipe pulled his KA-BAR knife out and put it close to the monster's eye.

Monster: "I need a medic. My face is swollen. A spider bit me."

Phillipe: "OK, fair trade. Give me the class, and we pass, and I give you your boy."

Master Chief: "Rainbird, this is serious. Let him go now!"

Phillipe: "Live exercise. What happens happens. Your words."

Master Chief: "I'll court-martial your ass!"

Phillipe: "I'm willing to let him die. Are you?"

Master Chief: "Secure from exercise. Rainbird, you fuckin' asshole, get down here ASAP!"

Nahlense and Sonny were eating breakfast when the two detectives interrupted. All Nahlense saw was a badge at first, and then they introduced themselves as Canaby and Barnes. Nahlense thought that shit sounded like a fuckin' TV show, but when they asked both of them to come to headquarters to answer a few questions, he obliged.

Once they arrived downtown, Nahlense sat in a room for about two hours, waiting. Same shit, different day. No matter what state he'd gone to, the fuckin' cops' playbook was the same shit.

Canaby walked in and sat down. The senior detective established that he knew who Rufus Jackson was. Born in Pearl River, Louisiana, April 30, 1939, mother Sadie, father Rufus Sr., both deceased, three brothers, all incarcerated at Angola. Rufus had served five years for possession, was not on parole, and his current address was known.

Canaby asked, "What business do you have with Trace

Strong?"

Nahlense said, "Mr. Strong is a friend."

Canaby knew this fucker was a graduate of gladiator school. No way he was going to say shit, so Canaby resorted to veiled threats.

"OK, Mr. Jackson, you can go, but Big Trace is going down. And if you're with him, so will you."

Nahlense smiled while standing, showing every gold tooth in his mouth, and said, "Yes, sir."

September eleventh, 9:00 a.m., Coronado Island, California. BUD/S graduation was bittersweet. These were guys that Phillipe had spent eighteen to twenty-four hours a day with for the last six months, most of them. He probably would not see them again. Also, Michele could not come because invitations were limited to two guests, and Phillipe's parents are coming. When Phillipe had called his father and told him the good news of his graduation, his father had said, "OK, but how do I tell your mother?"

It had completely slipped Phillipe's mind that he'd never told Moms. Oh shit!

Willie Rainbird was a small business owner, so getting time off wasn't an issue, but Mary had to pull some last-minute strings. So the Rainbirds were off on their first road trip in years. Their conversation was awkward at first, but it slowly softened to the point where both started to ask and comment on each other's personal life.

When they got to Oceanside, they made a scheduled stop to eat breakfast. Willie, always the gentleman, opened the door to the restaurant and both waited to be seated.

The waitress escorted them to a table. The breakfast moved forward to the part where Willie began to explain to Mary the details of Phillipe's new job. After finishing, Willie saw an unfamiliar look on the face of his ex-wife. Mary's expression was one of anger, disappointment, and shock. It was the look she gave Willie that scared him because him could not predict what she would do.

Mary took a deep breath before responding. "OK, I know I'm supposed to get angry, but I'm not. We've talked about this before. Phillipe is an adventurer and always has been. Nobody can keep him in a box. I want my son to be safe. It's so dangerous for black men, but I can't take his manhood away for my own selfishness."

Willie smiled and said, "I've been selfish, too, by not trusting your judgment. I want the best for my children and you. We should all take this opportunity to appreciate the time we have, not regret the time we've missed."

Edward and Helen were walking together through the vestibule of the Whittingham estate. It seemed majestic. The vaulted ceilings and marble floors were just as Helen remembered them as a child. The Whittingham family had made their fortune in South Africa, representing the government in international affairs. The Whittingham's law firm made millions, and even more in global investments. The billable hours generated from a country with vast natural resources and an internationally condemned racist state were enormous. And Edward was the heir to the throne, a position he relished and took great pride in. With his Oxford law degree, he felt invincible. Helen's mind wandered to Nana and if she was in need.

The first to greet the new couple was Edward's mom, Gertrude Whittingham. She wore a blonde wig and lots of makeup, and carried her usual glass of wine. Johnathan Whittingham, Edward's father, was second with warm greetings, and he made all introductions to various guests. Most of the guests in attendance were clients, with a few friends sprinkled in. The entire party was well catered. Helen met several family members, and they seemed receptive to her new status. Edward left Helen to speak to the ladies of the party who were becoming more curious about the nature of Helen's character.

After a lull in the interrogation, Helen glanced to Edward, who was having a spirited conversation with an unknown man. He was tall and good looking. Helen asked Gertrude to explain. Gertrude simply passed it off as lawyers bringing their work to the party. She also stated that if Helen was going to be part of the family, she would get used to them bringing their work to the party. But Edward was obviously upset, so Helen excused herself.

While walking away, she heard whispering and snickering. Her operative training took over, and she was determined to find out what the bloody hell was going on. Helen knew that Gertrude hadn't been all that fond of her since she was a child, but this was something else.

Graduating from BUD/S was a rare feat. It was easier to graduate from an Ivy League school. The facts were undeniable that less than one percent of American population joined the Navy, and one percent of those became Navy SEALs.

Before the ceremony, all the invited guests took a tour

through the Naval Special Warfare museum and learned about the history of the Navy SEALs. Once the graduation ceremony was over, the entire class was invited to a barbecue at Tolliver's house. It was the first time Phillipe's mother got a chance to talk to her son. Mary sent a calming vibe and said that she understood he was a man. She said how proud she was and to do whatever was necessary to come home. Phillipe's spirits were sky high. Michele came with her parents. The parents were introduced, and everyone had a wonderful time.

September thirteenth, 10:00 a.m., New Orleans, Louisiana. Rufus Jackson could feel the seasons change. He was better than any weatherman, and there was a definite change. But it wasn't the weather; it was his accountant, Percy Moore. Percy thought he was slick, so he started skimming money. Rufus and Sonny were watching the Moore family sleep for a while. Sonny had tied up the kids and put them in the closet. Rufus took his sawed-off 12-gauge double-barrel shotgun and jabbed Percy. In haste, he rolled over and turned on the lights to find his boss.

Percy's anger subsided when he saw the shotgun. His fear for his wife and children increased. Rufus made one statement: "NOBODY steals from me!"

Rufus squeezed both triggers and hit Percy in the upper chest with both barrels. Percy's body flopped without life to the floor. Percy's wife tried to scream but couldn't. Tears ran down her face as she looked at Sonny walking closer with his knife. Sonny Otis. His skill with a knife was well known throughout the Seventh ward. He cut her throat slowly. She fought up until her death.

Sonny stood and said, "You ready?"

Rufus thought for a moment and then replied, "Do them kids. No loose ends. Cool."

"Cool," said Sonny with a grin.

Helen Masters' training conflicted with her emotions. She could feel there was something wrong, but she thought her paranoia was insecurity. So, when in doubt, learn. During the party, she quizzed Edward about the argument, and he denied that anything was serious. Bollocks.

A part of her training was picking up cross talk while engaged in extracting information from someone else, which was useful in situations like parties. She talked to numerous people and learned quite a bit—like the tall good-looking chap was George Roper, a law school mate of Edward's. They'd shared a dorm room and had been inseparable. After college, Edward had gotten George a job at Whittingham and Chanel as an associate.

Helen started following George around the next day. Nothing strange happened until nightfall when he took a taxi to a gay bar and Edward showed up a few minutes later. Helen remembered the first night she and Edward had made love. There were problems with Edward's libido. Helen felt insecure that Edward didn't think she was good enough, but the relationship became easier as they spent more time together. For a young man of his age, Edward wasn't a sex machine, by any stretch of the imagination, but he was kind.

Helen decided to confront Edward and tell him that no matter what direction he wanted to take his life in, she would support him unquestionably, but just don't lie. Edward and Helen met for lunch in Brighton. She directed the verbal exchange toward the subject of his friend George. Edward's mannerisms betrayed his thoughts. He became nervous and defensive. Helen gave him the opening to confess with dignity, and he eventually admitted to a homosexual relationship with George. Helen felt she had invested a lot of valuable time in the relationship, and she wanted things to work. Edward promised that it was over and he was in love with her. That's all he needed to say. Besides, Helen had to report back to work and she wanted her mind clear.

 # Chapter 6

November second, 1981, 6:00 a.m., Brecon Beacons, Scotland, UK. CSM Morris Winston was looking at his orders for the tenth time. He knew the words on the paper wouldn't change, but it was a nice idea. Apparently, the North Atlantic Treaty Organization, or NATO, had decided that terrorism was actually a strategic threat to the West. Winston rolled his eyes in disbelief that it had only taken a decade of international plane hijackings, Munich Olympic Games incursions, and embassy take-overs to figure this shite out. Now the Yanks, who had fucked the dog on terrorism for years, had blessed SAS with their fuckin' presence. And the fucks didn't have the sense to send veterans; they sent wet fuckin' noses.

Helen Masters had a maternal opinion that was the opposite. Aren't children easier to teach than adults? We can help them help us. She had a point again, and it was becoming a habit. Helen had taken a small opportunity and carved out a spotless reputation as an operator, which was the highest compliment to a soldier. Winston looked at the order again and said, "Bollocks."

In square mileage, Fort Benning, Georgia, was the biggest military installation in the world. Military personnel from all NATO countries came to learn leadership, light infantry tactics, and sniping. But airborne was the largest school, with 150 to 200 men per month taking the leap of faith.

Phillipe had a thing for heights, whether it was climbing trees or eating dinner on the roof of the house. Traditionally, at some point and time during training, SEALs would fuck with the instructors, or black hats, by stealing the hat of the senior instructor while jumping out of the plane. At the beginning of training, Master Sergeant Wilson assured the class that no fuckin' squid fuckin' rust pickin' swabby would ever take his beautiful Smokey Bear hat!

Phillipe couldn't resist the challenge, especially after Sergeant Wilson had crossed the line with the rust picker comment. So, the night before the final jump, two "unknown" masked men sneaked into Wilson's billet, or dorm room, and stole his hat. The next morning, base security was alerted to the awful situation. It seemed that some unpatriotic fuck had put a pink dress on the statue of General Benning, including pearls, makeup, women's underwear, and matching purse. And perched on the head of the general was a beautiful black Smokey Bear hat. Apparently, all the security cameras had been disabled, and there were no witnesses.

The entire jump school class mustered for a good tongue lashing by the base commander. Sergeant Wilson, for some reason, thought the fuckin' Navy had done it. Lieutenant Tolliver, feeling offended, told Wilson that he should not make accusations without proof. And furthermore, the lieutenant could prove that it couldn't possibly have been the Navy. Simple— everyone in the Navy knows that a black hat clashes with a white purse. And the mystery was never solved.

After all the fun at Benning, the class was thrown a curveball. Instead of being divided into the two existing SEAL teams, the guys went to two newly commissioned teams. Before 1981, there were only two SEALs teams—SEAL One on the West Coast and SEAL Two on the East Coast. The Holloway commission offered several recommendations concerning the Navy's inability to conduct special operations, one of which was expansion. The Navy's post-

Vietnam policy of "let it wither on the vine" was no longer acceptable, especially under the new and more militarily aggressive administration. New standards were implemented in the SEALs qualifications: All SEALs must be free-fall-parachuting qualified. So, the class was assigned to the new teams named Three and Four. Phillipe was sent to Three.

The entire class was sent to Fort Bragg, North Carolina. The preliminary training was in the wind tunnel, or the dragon, which simulates the falling of the body. The trainee's job was to control the body in formation. All trainees had to show competence in ten days or they were removed from training. Phillipe's first four times in the tunnel were comical, to put it kindly. But he got the hang of it and quickly mastered the dragon. The qualification concluded at the Yuma proving grounds, where the class really jumped out planes all day and night for three weeks.

Phillipe called and wrote Michele as much as possible. He was on a West Coast team and would see her soon. The day after the final jump, another curveball. SEAL Three would report for joint NATO training at Herefort. Phillipe's friend Grew was assigned to Four, so he had to go to Panama, much to the displeasure of his wife, who had to quit her job and move.

So, the newly formed SEAL Team Three mustered in front of this shack in the rain. CSM Morris Winston introduced himself. "Welcome, Yanks, to the Beacon. As you can see, we are having some marvelous English weather. This is a modified SAS training evolution. The reasons for this are I don't have the fuckin' time for this shite, and secondly, I don't think you fucks are worthy of full training. As you can see, we have a lady in our regiment. She is Lieutenant Masters. She is a fully qualified SAS operator, something you cunts will never be. I strongly suggest you watch the shite that comes from your mouths because Lieutenant's bite is much worse than her bark."

The first time Phillipe Rainbird made contact with Lieutenant Helen Masters, he was finishing his last leg of the star pattern navigation. She was sitting with her feet up and drinking some hot tea, keeping count of the number of Yanks who didn't get lost. Two weeks of land navigation, up and down the mountain. Phillipe's number was blue three. Phillipe ran to the desk. Helen looked as if she hadn't a care in the world, and she grinned at the rather cute Navy SEAL.

Their exchange:

Phillipe: "Hello, Lieutenant. Blue three reporting."

Helen: "Roger that, blue three. You look tired, blue three. Would you care for a spot of tea?"

Phillipe: "Thanks, but no thanks, Lieutenant. As you know, we are not allowed to receive or ingest any food or drink that's not in the rucksack."

Helen: "Oh, I'm so sorry. It must have slipped my mind. Well, you're the first one here, so you can go over there and relax. Instructions to follow."

Phillipe: "Yes, ma'am."

Phillipe walked to the rest area and flopped down. Helen put her feet up. She watched him closely without directly looking at him. Phillipe was thinking about Michele and the new status of their relationship. In the distance, he heard footsteps.

Through the bushes appeared Carlito Cruz, or red five. He saw Phillipe sitting in the rest area and jogged to the desk where Helen sat. The two exchanged words. Helen smiled while batting her eyes, and Cruz started walking toward the rest area mumbling. Cruz looked up and said one word, "Bitch." He explained that she had flirted with him and then offered a friendly cup of tea, but he remembered that he would fail the training.

Cruz said, "Fuckin' bitch. Did she smile the pussy at you too?"

Phillipe said, "Dude, she's just doing her job. Like that guy who left before hell week was secured, she's fuckin' with you." Cruz nodded.

Phillipe knew how irritable people were when fatigue was involved, and then he noticed that the lieutenant was staring. There was something about her eyes. Helen had heard most of the conversation between blue three and red five, especially the word "bitch." Helen was always amazed that men didn't realize how audio-sensitive women were. She saw that blue three was looking at her with an intoxicating glare. She returned it for a moment and then looked away. She understood how unprofessional it was to stare, but she couldn't help it. He was very attractive.

SEAL Team Three spent the next thirty days at shooting school, a crash course in the art of firearms. The way SAS taught tactical shooting was truly an art form. They had mastered point shooting, the equivalent of what is seen on television westerns—no aiming through the firearm sights with one eye closed. Both eyes open, one lines the shot placement and one eye for target acquisition. The theory was complicated and took time to get used to, but it worked. Once it was perfected, the operator was capable of engaging multiple targets, or tangos.

Other skills that were learned were shooting with either hand, which required one to practice all the time, and placement. Head shots only, something that basic SEAL firearms training did not emphasize.

Helen found teaching rewarding. The Americans were eager to learn, but somewhat immature. After every comment Helen made, a young man named Jimbo had something smart to say, especially the uncalled-for statements about Helen's boobs. It got so bad that Helen had walked to Jimbo very casually and asked him to stop or just be a man and say what he wanted from her. Jimbo, being a self-described ladies' man, told her he would like to take her somewhere and fuck her brains out. Phillipe tried to stop him, but it was too late. Helen took her index and middle fingers and struck Jimbo in the trachea like a snake, which caused him to hyperventilate and pass out. The medical staff went to work on Jimbo, and Helen addressed the class with a smile.

"Gentlemen, you're here to learn how to become better at doing your job. This is not a port of call. It would be better for everyone concerned if all of you stopped thinking with your cocks. I think I speak for the entire directing staff. Now, if anyone else would like to express their sexual desires, step forward."

Helen stared down the entire class and continued. "Good. Back to work."

Phillipe raised his hand and said, "Ma'am, I respectfully request the proper instruction on how to perform the rattlesnake move you just demonstrated."

Helen didn't know what to say. She thought he had gall, and she told the class she'd promise to give extra instruction on hand-to-hand after class if Mr. Rainbird would volunteer to be the practice dummy. Phillipe stood at attention and responded, "Aye, aye, ma'am."

December fifteenth, 9:00 p.m., Las Vegas, Nevada. Randell Green, or Speedy, was a great hundred-meter track star. He was a part of the Strong family, but he'd had a free ride to the University of Southern California. Even the head coach of the football team had wanted him to try out, but on grad night, he got into a car accident and fucked up his knees. Now Speedy was one of Big Trace's best homies. But it wasn't enough. Speedy had greatness so close, and being a flunky in Big's family was bullshit. On top of that, Big wasn't sharing what was going on with the money, which was why Speedy was taking a meeting with Nahlense. Speedy was impressed with the way he handled himself around Big. Most people never manipulated Big into cutting a deal, but this nigga did it. So, Speedy's thinking was "Big is about Big, and I'm going to get mine."

Nahlense was staying at the MGM Grand in the high-roller suite with two high-yellow girls. Speedy didn't see Sonny. He told Nahlense how he felt and asked what he could do to help.

Nahlense sized him up and said, "I thought Big was yo man."

Speedy came back with, "That nigga is gettin' sloppy. I need to go my own way."

Nahlense was skeptical. Was this some kind of test or is this fool for real?

"So, what you want from me?" Nahlense cautiously

asked.

Smelling his opportunity, Speedy replied, "I run the whole West Coast for you. I got all the connections. These niggas is tired of Big's ass."

Still suspicious, Nahlense decided to put this nigga to the test and asked one question: "Who killed Bear?"

December twenty-third, 3:00 p.m., Herefort, UK. CSM Winston sat in his oversized chair contemplating the direction of the meeting in progress. The DS, or Directing Staff, was debating which of these bloody Yanks were top shelf. In front of Winston were the service records of all twenty blokes, seven of whom had no combat experience. A lot of names were batted about in a single evolution, but one name consistently came up—Rainbird. He outperformed his teammates in every capacity, even the veterans. On a scale of 1–10 Mr. Rainbird graded 9.0. Bloody good.

Helen was reading Phillipe's service record during the debate when a hard knock was heard. The door swung open, and Commander Jeff Barclay, SEAL Team Three commander, walked in with the assistant commander, Ensign Emory Roberts. Winston greeted both and gestured for them to take a seat. He measured his words before speaking.

Winston: "Before I start, I would like to say that I have been pleasantly surprised by the overall performance of your people. That being said, your vets were very disappointing. They didn't seem motivated. In my opinion, their physical conditioning was substandard. Now the good news. Some of your young people show great potential. We all agree that Mr. Rainbird was the best performer."

Ensign Roberts: "Even me?"

Sergeant Major: "Yes, even you, believe it or not. You have to understand some of your blokes haven't operated in years, and your training regiment is substandard. This shouldn't be looked at as a negative. Talented young people are hard to come by."

Barclay: "So now what?"

Sergeant Major: "Sir, it's your command. I was instructed to brief you, but if you want a suggestion, you can either do nothing or give Rainbird a hand job. Whatever you decide, please do it off my bloody base, sir."

After the sergeant major had given his reasons for picking Rainbird, the SEAL team commander was not impressed. He felt training was not a replacement for experience. Winston agreed but still invited Rainbird for a beer.

When Phillipe was told to go to The Pub, which was a private bar that only allowed in guys from the regiment, he thought it was a joke. When he got there, he listened at the door. He didn't see or hear anything wrong, so he knocked three times. The room went dead silent, and Phillipe went into SEAL mode. He put his hand on his switchblade. The door was opened slowly by one of the DS. The bar was smoky and smelled of stale beer. He signaled for Phillipe to come in.

Phillipe entered, walking carefully, and then everyone started to cheer. A guy put a mug of warm beer in his hand. And then Phillipe saw on the opposite side of the room Sergeant Major Winston and the beautiful eyes of Lieutenant Masters. His eyes became fixed upon her. Her dark hair was down, and she was wearing a pantsuit and lipstick. Phillipe knew she was unavailable in one way or another, but that didn't matter tonight because he probably would never see her again. So what the fuck.

Helen was surprised to see Mr. Rainbird in civilian clothes. His well-built form was accented by the jeans he wore. She thought his unusual pigmentation, a dark brick color, was very appealing. Helen had no real experience with black men, other than the occasional friendship, but there was something different about Mr. Rainbird.

Winston and Helen stood when Phillipe came to the table. They exchanged Merry Christmas greetings, and all of them sat down. They had a good laugh at the choreographed entrance, and Winston asked whether or not Phillipe knew why he was invited. Phillipe told both of them no, and the sergeant major explained that he wanted to make sure that Phillipe understood that special ops was a unique opportunity to make real difference in this world. Helen concurred with Winston's sentiments and gave Phillipe a letter of recommendation on SAS stationery. Phillipe expressed his thanks and appreciation, and they all toasted to the next level of success. Winston, being an old fart, excused himself to go to the toilet. Phillipe and Helen had a real conversation.

Phillipe: "So what's your first name?"

Helen: "Lieutenant. Just kidding. It's Helen."

Phillipe: "Where are you from?"

Helen: "You ask a lot of questions."

Phillipe: "That's the best way to get to know someone."

Helen: "Why do you want to know me?"

Phillipe: "Because you read my service records, and

the questions I'm asking are the same ones that you know about me."

Helen: "Brighton."

Phillipe: That's by the Channel, right?"

Helen: "Impressive. Just like Los Angeles. I do have one question. Why didn't you go to college? We saw your acceptance letters. MIT and Stanford. What happened?"

Phillipe: "My parents could not afford it. A letter of acceptance is not a promise of financial aid."

By this time, Winston had returned, grumpy as ever, saying, "What the fuck are ya two talkin' about, eh?"

Phillipe and Helen broke eye contact for the first time since Winston had left. Phillipe's response was, "The Lieutenant was counseling me on my future educational prospects."

Winston said, "Bollocks!"

That was Phillipe's cue to say good-bye, but Winston had one more thing to ask. "What kind of name is Rainbird, anyway?

"Phillipe said flatly, "It's better than calling yourself Pelican."

Helen's beer came through her nose, and Winston let out a hearty laugh. They said good luck instead of good-bye.

December twenty-three, noon. Gertrude oversaw

lunch preparations for her daughter-in-law. When the bell

rang, one of many servants opened the door and escorted

Helen to the dining area. Helen and Gertrude exchanged pleasantries and sat down for lunch. The conversation was an obvious pissing contest over the pecking order of Edward's love. Helen was clear about not getting between a mother and son's relationship; also, she indicated that Gertrude might have been a little overprotective. After hearing that, Gertrude was so enraged she insulted Helen's heritage and threatened not to accept any potential "darker" grandchildren. Her patience gone, Helen went for the jugular and loudly said that the wedding was off. While walking out of the front door, Helen exclaimed, "Gertrude, you need not worry about grandchildren. Your son's massive craving for sperm, he should be pregnant in no time at all!" Helen slammed the door so hard it made the mansion shake; watching in disbelief were the servants, who had never seen anyone, including Mr. Whittingham, best Gertrude in a verbal battle.

Gertrude's anger boiled until she screamed, "Get back to fuckin' work!"

December twenty-sixth, 1981, 4:30 p.m., Beirut, Lebanon. The jewel of the Mediterranean, an Arabian version of the French Riviera, where the rich and famous played. But like so many other third-world countries, like Cuba and Vietnam, the corrupt governments lead to a two-class system. Coupled with brutal security forces, this unwittingly left the door open for revolution. Of course, some of these revolutionaries were trained operatives of the Kremlin, and their communist goals turned into a proxy war with the West.

The American Central Command and the White House decided that the Beirut airport was a strategic imperative to keep open, so they sent the Marines. Naval Special Warfare Command, or NAVSPECWARCOM, seized upon the opportunity to get the new SEAL team some operational experience. As the team disembarked the plane, they saw the diversionary smoke that was released for all aircraft landings. The wind was whipping the surf into a frenzy. There was a bus waiting to transport the new arrivals to the "barracks." It was reinforced to be bullet resistant.

Phillipe took two steps on the tarmac, and instantly, he was targeted by sniper fire. For a moment, he hesitated to grasp the situation when the biggest black man he had ever seen ran toward him. Everything seemed to slow down. The unknown black man was screaming something, but the aircraft noise was deafening. With one hand, the black man grabbed Phillipe by the head and dragged him to a nearby jeep. He tossed Phillipe in the back like a rag doll. After Phillipe hit the floor of the jeep, he regained clarity and heard the black man say, "What the fuck is wrong wit yo ass! Don't you know shit? You just got here, and you about to get dead!"

Phillipe's youthful emotions took over. There was a mounted .50 caliber Browning machine gun with a belt-fed two-hundred-round box, or M2 or MA deuce. His training and his dick kicked into high gear. Before the big black man could finish what he saying, Phillipe had fed the belt through. Phillipe cocked, locked, and was rockin', three bursts aimed specifically at the rooftop. The sun was at his back, so he could see the muzzle flash from the sniper. The large black man was waving his arms around, trying to get Phillipe's attention. With extreme focus, Phillipe allowed for wind and the direction he was moving in and took a breath. He let off a barrage of lead in the direction of the sniper, causing the spotter to get up and run. Unfortunately for the spotter. he stood up into a .50 caliber bullet, and the sniper looked as if he'd been hit because of the arterial spray.

Phillipe started yelling, "I got 'em! I got 'em!"

By now everyone on the base could hear the large black man's words. "Cease fire, you stupid *fuck!*"

The large black man grabbed Phillipe, pulled him into the front passenger seat, and started to choke him, saying, "Don't you fuckin' move!"

The ride ended at the Marine barracks. There was an alert going off, and the Marines were manning their stations. The commanding officer, or CO, looked at the large black man and asked, "Master Chief, who broke the fuckin' cease-fire?"

Master Chief turned his head slowly toward Phillipe. The CO looked at Phillipe and quietly said, "Get your goat-smelling ass in my office now."

The walk to the CO's office was every enlisted person's nightmare, especially when that person had fucked up. Phillipe felt like shit when he entered the office. It was typical military style, with an outer office for a staff person to do administrative support and the main office. Phillipe knew to stand at attention, and all questions were rhetorical unless you were yelled at for not answering. Commander Barclay, the master chief, and the CO were in attendance. The meeting went forward:

CO: "My name is Colonel Molonsky, and who the fuck are you?"

Barclay: "Sir, this man is under my command. If anyone disciplines him, it should be me."

CO: "Really? Did you brief this man on the cease-fire?"

Barclay: "No, sir."

CO: "Aren't you required to brief your men prior to landing?"

Barclay: "Yes, sir."

CO: "Well, no wonder he's a fuckup! Get the fuck outta my office. I'll deal with you later."

Barclay: "Yes, sir!"

CO: "Master Chief Tomlinson, how could you let this shit happen?"

Master Chief: "I don't make excuses, sir. If you want to know what happened, ask the source."

CO: "OK, Petty Officer Butt Fuck, what happened?"

Phillipe: "I was shot at. I returned fire, and I got them."

CO: "Oh, is that right? How do you know?"

Phillipe: "I saw it. One in the back and one in the face."

CO: "Bullshit. Did you see it, Master Chief?"

Master Chief: "No, I was driving, but the sniper fire stopped."

CO: "Stop covering him, Master Chief. Let's wait for the advance reconn team to come back before we court-martial this fuck! I should come over there and skull-fuck you right now."

Phillipe: "Sir, with all due respect, you just threatened me. Now, I take full responsibility for my actions, but if you come from behind that desk, I'm going to break my foot off in your ass, sir."

At this point, the conversation broke down to threats, and the master chief stepped in between them. Master Chief grabbed Phillipe, again by the head, and threw him out of the office, saying in a commanding voice, "Sit in the hall and *wait.*"

Phillipe gathered himself and his pride in the hallway. There was a hard wooden bench. Phillipe sat on it thinking to himself how all his hard work had been for nothing. Out of the corner of his eye, he saw a guy with long blonde hair and a beard. He seemed completely out of place, standing in the doorway of something called the Liaison Office.

In this purified jarhead world, he casually walked over and sat down. He offered Phillipe a cigarette, which was declined. The conversation between the master chief and CO was heating up. Phillipe glanced over at Blondie, who said, "Is that about you?"

"Yes," Phillipe replied.

Master Chief exited the office and gave the old "get the fuck over her now before I kick your black ass" gesture. Phillipe got up and reluctantly started to follow Master Chief, but not before Blondie said, "Bye bye. Nice talking to you."

Phillipe thought, "Great. I haven't seen my girlfriend in months, my career is ruined, and I'm being hit on by fags. Just fuckin' beautiful."

Once Phillipe disappeared, Blondie, or Major Timothy Corran of the United States Army, moved into action by entering the CO's office while he was distracted. As soon as the CO saw the major, he waved him away, saying that he had no time for "Liaison," or whatever bullshit the spec ops were calling themselves. T.C. sat down anyway and inquired about the young man who had caused so much trouble.

The CO explained details of the altercation as an example of youthful arrogance. The CO indicated that he rather liked the young man's moxie and take-no-prisoners attitude, but his insubordination could not be tolerated, so he had go to the mess decks on the USS John F. Kennedy.

T.C. allowed the exchange to calm down before asking whether or not the recon teams had reported back. CO said, "Preliminary reports are two bodies found, one Russian-made SVD sniper rifle, and some of the neighbors tried to steal and move the bodies. One shot in the back and one head shot. Jesus, the kid was right. He did get 'em."

T.C. immediately stood up and walked downstairs.

Master Chief Frederick Douglas Tomlinson was a thirty-year career man. He had started as a young marine, landing at Inchon during the Korean War. When advancement was hard to come by and the White House started to donate more money to special operations, he transferred to the Navy SEALs. After two tours in Vietnam, he was on his last deployment, and now he was babysitting some pissant to mess decks—a place where officers send young men to learn how to wait tables for six months. The reasons vary, but if the leadership had a problem person, the mess decks became punitive.

For Phillipe, like most people, the first time on an aircraft carrier was intimidating. The sounds of the arresting gear, jets taking off, and the rumble of the propulsion equipment all at once was overwhelming. The awesomeness of the ship was taken down a notch when Phillipe got to the mess deck, which was basically a cafeteria. Cleaning didn't mean shit to Phillipe. His grandmother was a maid and janitor. So there was no problem, but he entered the division officer's office, which he thought was pathetic. What kind of shitty officer is in charge of cleaning up a cafeteria? And sure enough, the rat bastard that was in charge was just that—he actually looked like a rat.

Lieutenant Junior Grade Dick Harris stood about five feet five inches and had a long pointy nose. He greeted Master Chief while ignoring Phillipe. All three went into the office. The rat sat behind his desk, and after a few minutes of pleasant banter, he looked at Rainbird.

"You know why you're here?"

Rainbird simply said, "Yes, sir."

"Good. So don't ask me when you're leaving like these other shitheads. That's all they send me is shit. Your job is the night crew supervisor. All the screw-ups are on nights. If I catch you or them fuckin' off, I'll write you up. Now your shift starts in an hour. Turn to."

When Master Chief docked the raiding craft, T.C.

was waiting on him to know how things had gone. They exchanged information and opinions about the young SEAL. T.C. decided to adjourn the debate to the Liaison office.

The major's Liaison office was a converted storeroom, ironically enough, because this was the unofficial office of the Activity. The Intelligence Support Activity, or ISA, was one of many units born from the ashes of Operation Eagle Claw, and the most successful. All the other units involved with that fiasco had suffered human and material loses, but Activity operated flawlessly. During Eagle Claw, the Activity was referred to as Field Operations Group, but when it was commissioned to be a permanent unit, the name was changed.

Major Tim Corran had spent most of his fourteen years in the Army with special forces. During his third tour, he was transferred to the Phoenix project and received his commission. He met Master Chief Tomlinson while practicing for the unsuccessful raid on the Son Tay prison camp to rescue American POWs. Now in the epicenter of terrorism, ISA was responsible for counterterrorism intelligence, but they didn't have any human intelligence. That was about to change. T.C. and Master Chief both sat down to process what had transpired. After a short period of time, they agreed that they needed to find more information about Rainbird.

Saul Wyman got his flash orders, and he was on the airplane for Los Angeles. He had to read the order on the way. "My God," he thought, "What was so important that he had to stop everything?"

Warrant Officer Wyman was the best background investigator at ISA. His job was profiling. He understood the type of individual who could have a great chance at being an efficient intelligence operative. Once he studied the acquired service records, he had a fundamental idea who he was dealing with. The file said Rainbird, Phillipe Sebastian. All Wyman really needed was basic information. His job was assessment. The important questions that had to be answered would not come in a file.

After the plane landed at LAX, Wyman collected his luggage and caught a shuttle to rent a car. He drove to the Marriott hotel, where he had a reservation. The room was clean and roomy for a single. The key to background investigation was to communicate with people who wanted to help the principal, or Rainbird—friends and family who had known this kid from day one. So, Wyman knew he couldn't come off like a cop and definitely not like an intelligence operative working for a clandestine unit. It was for these reasons that he had a multitude of identities and disguises. Wyman would visit the parents first. Once Wyman read the file, he knew exactly who he would impersonate to get everyone talking—a recruiter from Massachusetts Institute of Technology.

The law offices of Whittingham and Chanel were perfectly situated in the heart of London's business and financial hub. The wealth generated was evident by the lavish décor. Jonathan Whittingham's corner office view was spectacular. The Thames River and Big Ben were clearly visible. The huge oak desk was polished to a high sheen and sat in front of the panoramic windows. It did not matter whether it was day or night when Mr. Whittingham sat behind his desk. It was a visual representation of his power. As he sat in the visitor chair awaiting his father's lecture, Edward thought, "One day this will be mine."

"My son, I have big plans for you. I want to leave this firm to you, but you're becoming a bloody embarrassment. Now, your mum and I want grandchildren, and we think Helen is a good sort. So stop fuckin' about and get on with it."

Mr. Whittingham stopped for the point to sink in before continuing. "I want you to be happy, and I want you to be a bloody man. I recognize that you can make your own decisions, but I will not have this firm's business jeopardized because you want to take it up the fuckin' ass. We're an international firm with clients who still think it's the third century and will not fraternize with anyone who is homosexual. And by extension, that puts you in a position of weakness when the board is going through the confirmation process. Do you understand?"

Edward knew his father had never accepted him for who he was. Feeling castrated, he looked down at the floor, searching for the strength to fight back. He looked up and said, "Yes, father."

Chapter 7

December thirtieth, 6:30 p.m., Torrance, California. The dinner crowd at Norm's Restaurant was hectic. The Rainbird family sat patiently waiting for the recruiting officer from MIT. When Mary Rainbird had received the call at her job about the possibility of her son attending one of the most prestigious universities in the world, she had organized and ordered Willie to be present. The name of the recruiter was Saul Weintraub, and he was the chance that Mary had prayed for.

Mr. Weintraub walked in. He greeted Mary and Willie with a smile. He was taller than Mary imaged, well dressed and with a great sense of humor. Willie grilled Mr. Weintraub about financial specifics while Mary answered some questions about Phillipe's childhood.

One peculiar subject that was sensitive for Mary to discuss was Phillipe's juvenile record. The Rainbird family didn't like talking about the incident, but the recruiter said he would find out eventually. So, she told the story.

Mary: "I had just gotten a divorce, and I was trying to move on with my life. I met a man who seemed nice, but like myself, he had just gone through a nasty breakup. We dated for a while, and the relationship between us became strained. He wanted marriage, and I didn't. So I ended it, and we were just friends. To make ends meet, my brother moved in, and everything seemed OK. First, he started to call all the time, and then he started to show up at my house uninvited. My brother tried to talk to him, but he wouldn't listen. One night, he got drunk, and at three o'clock in morning started to bang on my door. I didn't want to call the police, so I tried to talk to him. He got angry and kicked in the door. My brother ran to protect me, but my ex-boyfriend knocked him unconscious. He was yelling at me, and all of a sudden there was a loud noise, and my ex fell to the ground. There was blood everywhere. I turned, and my son was holding a rifle. By this time, the neighbors had called the police, and they took my son to jail."

Mary's face was soaked with tears, and Willie comforted her. Saul asked whether or not the DA had prosecuted. Willie told him no. They determined it was self-defense. Saul apologized for any inconvenience and paid the check. He gave them a business card and told them he would be in touch. He walked to his car thinking, "Man, this kid is something else. I have to see that police report."

Helen's vacation was going in the same direction as her mood—in the toilet and swirling. She assessed the totality of her situation: Edward was gay, at best bisexual. Mr. and Mrs. Whittingham were obsessed with having grandchildren. Gertrude was a bigot and didn't want Helen to work. She had a burgeoning career that none of them give a shite about.

Nana was resting. Her endurance in doing the simplest of things was painful to watch, but she had made some progress. Her ability to communicate continued to improve, but walking was problematic, even with assistance. Helen's time with Nana was mutually beneficial. Nana's spirits lifted when Helen was around, and Helen felt comfortable in normal surroundings.

Edward's visit to Brighton was predictable. Helen's mentality toward him conflicted with her emotions. They sat down together, as they had done so many times before, but now the two were on different paths, and Helen had decided that their relationship should be put on hold until Edward chose a life. Their hearts and spirits were heavy with the disappointment of missed opportunity, though they still loved each other. Helen spent the New Year with Nana and went back to work.

Saul Wyman made his appointment with the Department of Children Services the day after dinner with the Rainbirds. The only thing more uncooperative than the bureaucracy were the clerks. After running through the bureaucratic maze, they informed Saul that the file he'd requested was unavailable because the LAPD had checked it out. Saul politely asked by whom, and the clerk said by Detective Adam Canaby. When Saul wanted to know why, the clerk said that it wasn't her job to keep up with what the police did. Saul timidly asked for the detective's location, and the clerk graciously complied.

Before Saul arrived at LAPD Venice division, he made some phone calls and pulled some strings to get a meeting with Canaby. Naturally, Saul had to wait a while before the meeting. He sat in the lobby area clearing his mind. He had to fool an experienced cop. The Rainbirds had been easy because they wanted to believe, but Canaby was trained to detect lies. So, Saul had to be at the top of his game by using a form of meditation that focused the mind on a single thing— becoming, not playing, a character.

Detective Barnes escorted Saul to the meeting room. Everyone was pleasant. They all sat down.

Canaby: "So, Mr. Weintraub, you must be a very important person. The chief called me personally."

Saul: "Well, Detective, MIT is a very prestigious institution with a lot of political connections. I apologize if you were inconvenienced."

Canaby: "No, not at all. Here are the records."

Saul: "Why do you have these, if you don't mind me asking?"

Canaby: "It's an open investigation, and I'm not at liberty to say. What do you know about Mr. Rainbird?"

Saul: "I know he's a great student. He did quite well on his SATs. Nice family, and he's in the Navy."

Canaby: "Who told you about his juvie record?"

Saul: "His parents. But they said there wasn't a conviction."

Canaby: "There never is with Mr. Rainbird.

Saul read the police report:

"The police were summoned to the Mary Rainbird home at 3:00 a.m., 3rd of February. Upon arrival, the officers saw one man lying on the front lawn from an apparent GSW to the lower right extremity. The man was identified as Kenneth Rivers, 40 years of age, from Los Angeles. The alleged assailant was Phillipe S. Rainbird, age 10. Mr. Rivers forcibly entered the home of Mary Rainbird and attacked the Rainbird family until being shot. Police questioned Phillipe Rainbird, but all he said was "Lawyer." Mr. Rivers was asked by officers how he got outside of the house. Mr. Rivers said he was dragged out by Phillipe S. Rainbird. Mr. Rivers refused to press charges."

Saul Wyman had been doing background checks for almost a decade and had never come across a guy like this. This Rainbird had "operator" written all over him. After reading the police report, which was a copy, Wyman placed it in a yellow folder and exited the room. Canaby tracked him down and asked Saul for an opinion. He said, "I don't condone Phillipe's actions, but I try to walk a mile in someone's shoes before I judge them."

Canaby, feeling less than convinced, acknowledged his wisdom and said good-bye. Barnes walked up from behind and asked what Canaby thought. He whispered while memorizing Saul's license plate, "Check him out."

January third, 1982, 12:00 a.m., USS John F. Kennedy. CE3 Phillipe Rainbird was teaching a class in trigonometry to the "shit" he was supervising. Phillipe had spent the last two weeks trying to prove Lieutenant Rat Face wrong while still doing an exceptional job of cleaning. In his zeal to catch someone doing something wrong, Rat Face showed up during one of the classes and had a hissy fit. He threatened to write up everybody and court-martial Rainbird.

Phillipe calmly explained that Navy regulations stated that training classes during working hours was acceptable as long as it did not affect the workload. Rat Face turned into a cute red-faced bitch and started to tell Phillipe he wasn't scared of him, so don't try the intimidation shit. Phillipe was really trying hard not to laugh at this punk muthafucka, and the conversation ended with Rat Face storming out of the mess decks to tell the captain of the ship.

Captain Peter Henderson's record was impeccable—
top of his class 1966, fighter pilot, Vietnam '68–'71, and on a
fast track to admiral. So he didn't hold Lieutenant Harris in
high regard, but he had a job to do. Harris asked for permission
to enter the captain's stateroom, and permission was granted.

"Sir, I have a problem with one of my people. He is
insubordinate, and I want him to go to captain's mast."

"Really, you can't handle a mess deck worker?"

The captain's sarcasm was tempered by the knowledge
of who he was talking about. Major Corran had already
briefed him on Mr. Rainbird and requested that the captain
be prepared. Besides, pilots and SEALs have a great working
relationship. Not wanting to seem weak, Lieutenant Harris
started to scramble to make excuses, and the captain, growing
tired of Harris's belly aching, told him that he would take
care of it.

Feeling vindicated, Harris marched down to mess
decks to gloat. When the captain showed up and did an
informal walk-through and did not see any discrepancies, he
found the infamous Petty Officer Rainbird. After watching
his training regimen, the captain was more than impressed.
He asked for a word in private.

The captain explained that Phillipe was doing a good
job, but asked why the need to piss off Harris? Phillipe said
his intent was to mentor and provide guidance. He couldn't
understand why anyone in a leadership a position would
think that what he was doing was wrong. The captain agreed
unofficially and told Phillipe to carry on.

Several hours later while Phillipe was grading some
homework papers, he heard footsteps approaching and

looked up to see Blondie. Phillipe exhaled to gather himself and his thoughts. Why the fuck was he here?

Blondie said hello and sat down.

Phillipe: "What's up?"

Major: "I heard you were down here, so I came by to say hi."

Phillipe: "Hello. Good-bye."

Major: Do you mind if I have a word?"

Phillipe: "Yes, I do mind."

Major: "Wow, you seem really eager to sweep the floor. I guess it's what your grandmother taught you."

Phillipe: "Who the fuck are you?"

Major: "I'm sorry I didn't introduce myself. Here's my ID."

Phillipe: "Timothy Corran, Major, United States Army. So this ain't the Army, Major. What do you want?"

Major: "You."

Phillipe: "Look, sir. Your business is yours. I'm not with the faggot shit. Get your ass off my mess decks, sir."

Major: "Stand down, sailor. Now, if you don't want to spend the time you have left in the Navy sweeping floors and shuffling, get your ass to the flight deck. Now.

Phillipe could not believe this white boy. He said, "Yes, sir. I'll be there in five."

His anger boiled over. Phillipe tried to control it,

but it was too late. The major was about to get cut a new asshole. Phillipe walked into the galley, or kitchen, found the sharpest knife, and palmed it securely. He ran up five decks until he felt sea breeze on his face for the first time in two weeks and realized how much he had missed freedom. All air operations were suspended because of the cease-fire, but all aircraft were prepped to go. He walked between some planes, and the major appeared.

Major: "I have a job for you."

Phillipe: "Oh, yeah? What, sir?"

Major: "Working for me."

Phillipe: "Doing what?"

Major: "What fuckin' difference does it make? You won't be using a mop, and you'll be using all those hard-earned skills."

Suddenly, Phillipe got a vibe that an opportunity was presenting itself. He started to relax and decided to hear the major out, but keep his distance. They walked toward the bow, or front, of the ship.

Major: "I work for the Activity. Ever heard of it?"

Phillipe: "No."

Major: "Good. The less people who know the better. The Intelligence Support Activity is responsible for gathering all three facets of intelligence concerning counterterrorism, but we also have a mission opportunity statement. Which is where you come in."

Phillipe: "What do you mean?"

Major: "That's classified. I've got to know you're on

board first."

Phillipe: "So, you're not the CIA?"

Major: "Fuck no. We exist because special ops was tired of getting fucked over."

Phillipe: "OK. Why me?"

Major: "Why not you? You doing something more important? In or out? Right here, right now."

Phillipe: "OK. I'm in. I don't need this knife anymore. I need to pack and check out in the morning."

Major: "You are paranoid. No need. It's already done. Follow me."

Phillipe was stunned. He followed the major to the center of the flight deck. There sat a brand-new UH-60A helicopter, or Black Hawk. Phillipe recognized it only because he'd read an article in *Popular Mechanics*. Only the Army had Black Hawks, and the Navy was years away from their acquisition. Phillipe was sold. This major must be legit. The pilots were holding a seminar with the flight deck crew about the space-age flying machine. Every time one of the pilots pressed a button, there were oohs and aahs, like kindergarten kids watching a magic show.

Phillipe saw his duffel and garment bags in the crew bay of the Black Hawk. What was disturbing was that his padlocks were on his duffel. All sailors were issued padlocks for lockers, and the only set of keys was around Phillipe's neck. So he checked both locks, and they opened.

Phillipe looked at the major and politely asked, "How'd the fuck did you open my locks, sir?"

The major grinned and said, "You're not the only one who can pick a lock."

Phillipe ignored the comment and inspected the contents of both bags, including his service records that the major possessed. Once finished, Phillipe indicated that he was ready, and the pilots did their preflight checks. Then they took their seats. Before they were given clearance to take off, the major said to Phillipe, "Tell about me Bear."

Vaughn Sykes wasn't a typical criminal. His family was like a television show. His father worked as an executive for an aerospace company, and his mom was a homemaker. Sykes had gotten the best education money could buy. At the tender age of sixteen, his parents bought him a sports car. He had everything a kid could want, except being down with the set, or street cred. This was more perception than reality because it was based on what you had done or what you could do. If the homies on the block thought you were cool, then you were cool. If they didn't know or see you on the block hanging out, then you were not cool.

Sykes had great parents, and they were only concerned for their son's long-term welfare. They didn't give a goddamn about what some ignorant niggas' opinions were. But, the peer pressure to be accepted was too much for Sykes to handle. So he started with nickel-and-dime shit. In a short period of time, he stepped up to taking custom orders from Big, and that's exactly where Nahlense wanted him—close enough to fuck shit up when the time was right.

Sykes drove up in a pickup truck to Big's Hollywood Hills home. Huey and Speedy were in the driveway smoking a joint. Sykes got out of the truck with an obvious overt attempt to be accepted. "Hey, man. What's up? What y'all doing? That shit smells good than a muthafucka! Let me hit, that nigga!"

Huey stood up slowly and said, "Nigga, shut the fuck up! I'll let you smoke this if you don't say shit else."

Not wanting any part of Huey, Sykes took the joint and didn't say another word. Giggling at how much of a punk Sykes was, Speedy walked to the truck and pulled back the canvas covering to see the brand-new Altec studio equipment. Speedy told Huey this was some nice shit, and Huey nodded. Looking in the eyes of Sykes, Huey told him to take the joint and his ass the fuck outta here. Sykes slid silently into the vehicle, started the engine, and drove off toward Laurel Canyon. When he got to Sunset Boulevard, he found a telephone booth and made a call.

Nahlense: "Yeah."

Sykes: "Hey, baby. It's me, your boy."

Nahlense: "OK."

Sykes: "I dropped that shit off. I think they liked that shit."

Nahlense: "Cool. I thought they might. Good job. Oh, by the way. Next time you call, act like you got some damn sense." Dial tone.

March twenty-seventh, 6:45 p.m., Al-Aqsa Mosque, Jerusalem, Israel. Evening prayers in the Muslim religion are about communion and submission to Allah, blessed be his name. Neighbors, family, and friends participate in a beautiful act of love and devotion to one's creator. Husam El Qismat had been coming here since he was a little boy. This was a place of peace and brotherhood. His occupation was something else.

Husam was a very successful international arms smuggler. He didn't pick sides, though most of his business came from the Muslim freedom-fighting organizations. Husam's political views were moderate compared to some of the Muslim brethren because he had spent time in the West. After his father was killed by radicals for voicing his opinion of negotiations over violence, his mother moved the family to Brooklyn, New York. Husam and his sister, Zubaida, both went to NYU. At school is where he connected with some of the faithful. He used his head for business to carve out a plan to provide whatever was needed and to remove all competition.

Husam met his bodyguards at the car. He didn't know their names, and there was no need to. Money bought their loyalty. The new 500SEL Mercedes sped through the streets of Jerusalem. When a black van cut them off, the Mercedes-Benz swerved to avoid the collision. The van abruptly stopped, and the back doors swung open. Two men with AK-47s started firing, killing the bodyguards instantly. Husam quickly exited the car.

Husam heard men yelling at him in French to stop. He ran several blocks and scaled many fences until he came upon a taxi. Husam pulled out his CZ 75 pistol, approached the driver, who was sleeping, put the muzzle firmly to his head, and said in Arabic, "Help me and you will be rewarded, or die."

The rather young man replied, "Yes," and started the old BMW. Husam climbed in the back, and they took off. The driver asked where he should go. Husam asked his name, and the driver replied, "Abdul," in a frightened voice. Seeing the fear, Husam assured him that everything was OK. The cab came to an intersection, where two black vans blocked them. Men wearing black masks and speaking French ordered both occupants to get out of the car. Husam and Abdul were put on their knees, handcuffed, and gagged.

The ride in the back of the van answered a lot of Husam's questions. Number one—who were these people? From the cross talk, he gathered they were DST, or Directorate of Territorial Surveillance, the French version of the CIA. Husam knew that this was not good. The DST had been looking for him a long time, but he had managed to evade detection. Someone must have talked. He knew his organization was compromised, and if he escaped, his wrath would be unbridled.

The van stopped. Husam and Abdul were dragged out and forced into some building. They walked down some stairs, into a room, and were pushed into chairs. Their hoods were removed, and Husam got a good look at Abdul, not knowing he was looking at Phillipe Rainbird. His beard and hair had grown several inches the last three months since he decided to get on that helicopter.

The major and Phillipe had a conversation on the Black Hawk that was full of half truths and denials. Phillipe had learned from the best, Willie Rainbird and Trace Stong. Rule number one was never trust anybody, especially white people. Rule number two was no confession, no case. Phillipe could not believe the major was trying to get him to admit to a capital crime. The major asked the same question a hundred different ways, and Phillipe gave the same three answers: "I don't know," "I don't remember," and "Lawyer."

When the major wondered why Phillipe didn't trust him, his reply was, "I don't trust nobody, including myself. If my right hand goes into my pocket to get a quarter, my left hand is waiting to search him to make sure the muthafucka ain't stealing."

The major replied, "If you don't trust me, why are you here?"

Phillipe told him that people would always gravitate to their own self-interest, no matter how benevolent it started out. And whatever the major's motivations, Phillipe was getting what he wanted.

After a long pause in the conversation, Phillipe and the major went to sleep. An hour had passed when the pilot communicated that they were landing in fifteen minutes.

When the copter set down, the dust was blinding. Several men escorted them to a building with unusual writing on it, and some of the men spoke a language that Phillipe did not understand.

They turned the corner to a bank of freight elevators with a numeric lock. Everyone entered and descended. There were no indications of how far, but Phillipe counted to fifteen before the elevator stopped. It opened up to a vast underground facility and a pretty lady in a military uniform. She welcomed the foreigners and ordered them to follow. Phillipe realize that she was Israeli military. They entered a large room, and there were six people sitting quietly, observing.

Everyone greeted the major as though they were old

friends. One old man walked over to Phillipe to shake hands. The old man introduced himself as Colonel Abe Cohen and said this was a Mossad facility.

Colonel: "Mr. Rainbird, I've heard so many interesting things about you, I almost thought you were a myth."

Phillipe: "Really. For instance?"

Colonel: "Well, I heard you are smart, tough, and innovative. Is that true?"

Phillipe: "It might be. What do you want?"

Colonel: "Right to the point, I see. We are running a joint operation with the ISA. It's in the most dangerous place in the world, Lebanon. We are looking for a dark-skinned undercover operative who can live for months speaking the languages—Arabic, French, etc. The operative should be young and athletic and possess a mentality that is conducive with violence. Now, from the information we have collected about you, I would say you're that guy."

Phillipe: "So, you want me to be a spy?"

Colonel: "Well, that's not how I would put it, but OK."

Phillipe: "So, why me?"

Colonel: "You see, Phillipe. Can I call you Phillipe?"

Phillipe: "Yes, Abe."

Colonel: "Certain attitudes exist in all cultures. Now, we try to exploit those attitudes to our advantage."

Major: "Basically, Arabs have a history of prejudice against black people and look at them as subservient."

Phillipe: "OK. And because I'm black, it will be easier for me to be invisible, or subservient, as you say."

Major: "Told ya he was smart."

Phillipe: "Yes, he is. What's in it for me?"

Colonel: "He's a capitalist too. You didn't tell me that. What do you want?"

Phillipe: "Half a million dollars, half now in a Swiss bank account."

Major: "Or we just send you back to being a maid."

Phillipe: "Fuck it. Let's go, sir. I'm sure there are millions of black guys around that speak multiple languages and have a knack for survival. And let's not forget expendable."

Colonel: "One hundred thousand dollars, not a penny more."

Phillipe: "Deal. When do we start?"

March twenty-seventh, 9:00 p.m., Catalina Island, California. Willie and Mary Rainbird had spent the last two days together, the first in years. After the divorce, they had gone their separate ways and both thought about marriage to other people. But, they had always been friends, though their immaturity and lack of understanding eventually led to a breakup. Now, wiser and more patient, the Rainbirds started to appreciate each other for who they were, not who they were not.

The weekend trip to Catalina Island was romantic and fun, and they talked endlessly about the future. The island restaurants were five-star. They rented a little house on the top of a hill. The views were breathtaking, and the passion that had been dormant for a decade made them both feel alive. Willie never wanted it to end. He had received the gift of perspective. A life without Mary was too much to bear, and in a rare moment of reckless, he uttered, "Will you marry me again?"

Mary said, "Yes. Again."

The irony of Phillipe Rainbird in prison was almost laughable if his long beard didn't itch so much. He had always been so careful, and now he was not only in prison, but on purpose. But not for long. Phillipe, or Abdul, was about to escape with Husam and get his Islamic street cred. Abdul had played the game right. The DST thought he worked for the Husam organization. T.C. and old Abe had used their contacts to falsifying a warrant for Andre Gacon, or Phillipe. After a fingerprint check, DST couldn't wait to slap him around and make accusations. Gacon's legend was tailored to convince DST that the coincidence of Husam just happening to get into a cab with a man who was former French Foreign Legion and wanted for drug trafficking was too convenient.

The holding cell was dark and damp. Since prisoners were chained, they had to wallow in their own waste. Inmates received three interrogations every day and no food. Husam was being interrogated, so Phillipe focused all his reserve strength on prepping his escape. First, he lifted himself into the standing position. He used his hands to reach under his chin and found some braided hair. He loosened the hair, and inside was a short lock-picking jim. He started to work the locks on both chains.

It took a little longer to work the cell door lock, but it eventually opened, and he closed it back. Phillipe heard the guard walking in the distance, so he ran back to put his chains on and did his best crucifixion imitation. One guard dragged Husam to his cell. His partner was shooting the shit with the guard at the front desk. Behind the front desk was an alarm button. Phillipe knew that he had to be stealthy.

When the guard was busy putting the chains on Husam, Phillipe snuck up behind him, and in one sharp blow to the base of the skull, the guard fell unconscious. Husam's one good eye looked up and saw Abdul, or whoever. A smile crossed his face.

After Husam was released, the two undressed the guard, and Phillipe whispered his plan in Husam's ear. Phillipe exchanged clothes with the guard. He could not believe that the guard smelled almost as bad he did. Husam put the guard into chains and shoved the guard's underwear into his mouth. Phillipe checked the guard's gear, handcuffs, radio, keys, and retractable baton, and then he made sure the hallway was clear.

Husam nodded to indicate he was ready to pretend to be sick and unable to walk. Phillipe carried Husam down the dark hallway yelling for help in French. The guard behind buzzed open the gate and came to assist. Phillipe came through the gate and tossed Husam at the desk guard. Once caught, Husam started to beat the guard senseless. Simultaneously, Phillipe unsheathed the retractable baton and attacked the other guard with four quick strikes to the face, neck, knee, and groin. The guard fell to his knees, and Phillipe administered a choke hold until the his body went limp.

Husam and Phillipe tied up the guards, and Husam changed into a guard uniform. Phillipe knew there was one camera in the hallway outside, and he needed a diversion, so he took the spare guard keys and threw them into the cells. Phillipe and Husam casually strolled out to the hallway where the camera was located. They talked in French about futbol. They avoided the area of the interrogation rooms. It was logical that the exit would be in the opposite direction.

They came upon a metal security door. After a moment of fumbling and trying to find the key, Allah smiled upon them, and the heavy door opened to a stairwell. There was another camera. They tried to cover their faces, and after three flights of stairs, there was another security door. Phillipe yelled in French to open.

They heard a loud buzzing, and they burst through to discover one old man with a pistol. Phillipe hit the old man on the hand that was reaching for the gun. There was a loud pop, and before the old man could scream, Husam punched him in the mouth. While Husam dealt with the old man, Phillipe looked for an exit, walking swiftly down the corridor to a door. There was a small window in the door. Phillipe inspected the door for alarms before peering through the window and seeing a parking lot full of black vans. Husam approached from behind and showed Phillipe some car keys, whispering, "The old man said these are the keys to a van."

Phillipe saw a guard smoking a cigarette with his back to him. Suddenly, the alarms started to go off. The guard threw down his cigarette and started running to the door. He opened the door and came face-to-face with Husam, holding a 9mm pistol. Husam shot him once in the head.

Phillipe and Husam got into the first van. Husam

started the engine and raced off into the night. When they headed west after they got their bearings, Husam said to Phillipe, "My friend, who are you really?"

Colonel Abe Cohen and Major Tim Corran watched helplessly from a building across the street as a DST agent was murdered in cold blood. T.C. had given Phillipe explicit orders not to kill or let Husam kill anyone. The French were their allies. How in the fuck could Rainbird let it happen?

The colonel took the liberty of answering the rhetorical question, stating that intelligence operations always went wrong. Abe had been in his business since World War II, and he had never seen or heard of a perfect op. Perfection was never to be trusted. It was the enemy's favorite bait to trap the ignorant or the lazy spy. The colonel surmised that because the escape required killing, it probably would form a bond between Husam and Phillipe. Besides, the Israeli government had tried for years to stop the DST from operating these safe houses. The colonel and the major looked on as prisoners started to run out of the building. The colonel radioed the police to arrest everybody.

April fourth, 5:00 a.m., Ascension Island, British Overseas Territories, South Atlantic Ocean. Nothing gets one's mind off one's personal problems like a good war, Helen Masters pondered. It would seem that on the second of April, 1982, the Argentinean government thought the best course of action was to invade two British territories—the Falkland Islands and South Georgia—to divert attention away from their own economic incompetence. The islands had been in dispute for over a century, and up until late March 1982, the United Nations had been mediating a settlement.

When the Prime Minister heard of the invasion, rumor had it, she tossed an ashtray across the room and told the Admiralty, "*Break* them, and within ninety days, if they don't surrender, *destroy* Buenos Aires!"

Helen grinned at the thought. Propaganda and politics were two peas in a pod. Her thoughts turned to family. She was missing the wedding of one of her American cousins and Gram's birthday. She hadn't been to America in so long. Of course, Nana's health was improving. Her physical therapy had progressed to the point that she was starting to walk again. The Sunday before Helen deployed, she had gone to church at St. Michael's and had a private word with Father Reilly. He promised to look after Nana. Helen's personal relationship with Edward was now platonic. The only positive was that Mr. Whittingham saw his son stand up for himself and take pride in being gay.

The SAS was preparing for a covert amphibious infiltration alongside the Special Boat Squadron. The British Navy was in charge, so the SBS had the point. Helen was attached to D squadron. Their job was to get eyes on the Argentinean forces, designate targets, and prep the battlefield for invasion. Simple. Of course, doing it without getting killed or captured was another thing.

The preparation was endless. Helen broke down a hundred reconnaissance reports and satellite photos. When she tried to get some rest, a weird thought crossed her mind and kept her awake. It wasn't fear but the face of Mr. Rainbird.

The Mediterranean Sea has an unusual odor and color that cannot be explained by pollution. Two thousand years of naval battles and the unclaimed dead resting at the bottom of the sea. They were no longer men or vessels, just small and insignificant pieces of sea to be recycled into food or shelter for the indigenous underwater life forms.

Phillipe, now Andre Gacon, was on an Ethiopian fishing trawler heading west. Husam had secured transportation from his international contacts, and he was on the shortwave radio to make sure everyone was paid. Phillipe watched him closely, to understand him. So far, Phillipe was impressed with his ability to get shit done. Husam was a brilliant businessman and had kept his word so far.

Phillipe was working on a fishing line on the port side aft when he saw a newspaper in French that was a couple of days old. The headline read, British Troops Invade Falkland Islands! The first thought Phillipe had was, "Where in the fuck are the Falkland Islands," and the second was, "I wonder if Helen is there." He took a moment to pray for her safety.

Husam sat down next to him and said, "British imperialism. Will it ever end? Andre, my friend, where will you go after Cypress?"

Andre said, "I have a wife in Beirut."

Husam shook his head in disapproval. He informed Andre that DST agents were everywhere and surely had his wife under surveillance. Andre agreed with that possibility, but said that with rebellion in full swing, they didn't have the manpower.

Husam asked him what he would do for employment, and Andre said he didn't have anything specific in mind, but he would survive. Husam grinned, saying, "Perhaps I can help."

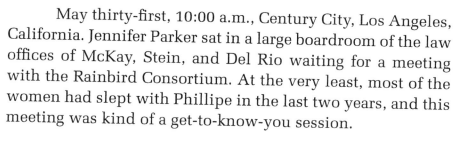

Chapter 8

May thirty-first, 10:00 a.m., Century City, Los Angeles, California. Jennifer Parker sat in a large boardroom of the law offices of McKay, Stein, and Del Rio waiting for a meeting with the Rainbird Consortium. At the very least, most of the women had slept with Phillipe in the last two years, and this meeting was kind of a get-to-know-you session.

Phillipe never bullshitted about commitment or the lack thereof, but when he floated the idea of Jennifer being the mediator and facilitator, her surprise was an understatement. So, Phillipe set up a preliminary meeting with Michele Matthews, and it went well after the initial insecurities were proved unfounded.

Jennifer and Michele were strong minded enough to understand that they had moved on, and the best thing for Phillipe was to go his own way without baggage. Besides, this meeting was about the one thing that trumped personal agendas—money. Phillipe had the foresight to realize that pure criminal or immoral activity was not a long-term solution to financial problems, but it could open doors to allow the disenfranchised a seat at the American-dream table.

When the participants filed in, Jennifer's feminist pride surfaced because everyone there was a woman. Granted, Phillipe had orchestrated the deal, but the women in the room had the power to kill it. Once the pleasantries were received and returned, the meeting started with introductions—Katherine McKay, attorney; Edith Stein, attorney; Donna Sanchez, McDonald's franchisee; Lisa Carter, resorts; Lynette Abate, real estate development; Michele Matthews, CEO of Genesis investments; and Jennifer Parker, a representative of

Apache Investors offshore hedge fund.

Michele stood and said, "I'd like to thank everyone for being here, and because Phillipe's parents are getting married again this weekend, this is a real busy week. Without further delay, we are here to pool our resources. We can be regionally successful, or we can be internationally recognized, by not only expansion in our present ventures but diversification into all aspects finance, real estate, and hospitality. We can make history by being the only all-women conglomerate. Before I give my presentation, are there any questions?"

Lisa Carter stood up and said, "Yes, I have two questions. First, where do I sign up? And second, is Phillipe a stud or what?" The tension was lifted with laughter.

Helen Masters somehow was sleeping throughout the helicopter ride. When the body needs rest, a human being can sleep anywhere and anytime. Six weeks into the bloody Falklands War, and the progress was being undermined by British arrogance. The British government officials were over-promising and blaming the military for under-delivering.

The mission this morning was a recce on Mount Kent in East Falkland. Argentinean special forces, along with a support element, were trying to control the high, and the Admiralty wanted real-time intelligence. Helen was inserting with D squadron, twelve mates.

Helen's intelligence experience had come in handy in West Falkland. After infiltration by canoes, D squadron reconnaissance determined that heavy winds would comprise the invasion timetable by delaying air support. Helen suggested that SAS go back to its World War II North

Africa roots of attacking the Argentinean aircraft while they were grounded. This, by extension, would cause confusion while the primary forces would attack from the sea and air.

The Sikorsky Sea King rattled and shocked to a rough landing. When all twelve personnel disembarked the choppers, they flared out into positions with their heads down. The Sea King's lift-off was extremely noisy. Helen thought, "They must know we're here." When gunfire from automatic weapons lit up the night sky, one round nearly hit Helen in the head.

The last Sea King to take off took several direct hits, and black smoke started to pour from the engine. The pilot lost control of the spinning vehicle, slamming into the mountain in a deadly explosion. The commander of D squadron rallied and regrouped the team like an experienced professional would and went on the attack, breaking them up into four teams of three.

They pushed back the Argentinean forces, destroying a mortar emplacement. The armored vehicle that brought down the Sea King tried to escape, but the LAWS rocket Helen unleashed sent the vehicle tumbling and burning. Once D squadron had cleared the area, they pulled back to the highest ground and assessed the casualties.

Helen's medical expertise was at the forefront as she established a triage. The team members made camp by instituting a security watch, communications, and patrols. The commander called a section leaders' meeting and told everyone to be prepared for a second and a third wave of attacks before reinforcements arrived. When asked how long it would be, he answered, "However bloody long it takes. We will not relinquish our position."

Helen had a funny thought that she didn't share. It was only one word: Waterloo.

The morning sun scorched the city of Beirut. Even though it was only mid-spring, the temperature would be well into the nineties. Phillipe Rainbird had entered and left Cypress on a clean Canadian passport provided by the Husam El-Qismet organization and had stayed there for a few weeks. Husam was very generous, and Phillipe knew that he was being watched, so his daily habits were consistent with someone who was a tourist.

When Phillipe applied for a student visa to the American University of Beirut, the French consulate was shocked because no one was going there, and definitely not for tourism. After an hour or so of trying to convince the young college student that his educational plans were reckless and briefing him on all of the security procedures, they finally approved Khalid Abu Masud, aka Phillipe Rainbird.

The beauty of walking right through customs while being a wanted criminal with a fake identity was doing it with a smile. Phillipe hoped Abe's police raid would detain all DST personal and, at the very least, confiscate all documents relating to the Andre Gacon interrogation.

Phillipe's face was clean shaven. This would confuse most custom agents. He was dressed in very preppy attire— Polo shirt, Levi's jeans, and Nike jogging shoes. He passed through and caught a cab to the American, or green, zone of the city. He arrived at the Beirut Hotel.

In the distance, sporadic gunfire could be heard, but that did not stop the merchants from carrying on business as usual. As soon as Phillipe stepped out of the cab, he was rushed by ten or twelve people, mostly children, begging for change. Phillipe swung his knapsack over his shoulder and walked in the hotel, where two soldiers stopped him to search him. The outside of the hotel was riddled with small-arms fire, but inside was elaborate and reminiscent of a time when wealthy patrons who had graced the halls.

Phillipe was in the process of checking in when he saw a familiar face. It was Major Tim Corran, who was sitting in the bar chatting with an attractive lady. Phillipe wondered if the major's wife knew her husband was such a ladies' man. Their eyes made contact for a moment, and Phillipe walked up to his room. The second-floor room was average in size and below average in cleanliness, but that wasn't important. He would be leaving as soon as he hooked up with his contact.

Phillipe tried to relax in between mortar explosions. His mind wandered to his time in Israel, where he had learned spy tradecraft, a short and condensed version of a school that usually took years. The physical conditioning had been easy enough, but the mental games were exhausting because they never stopped. Phillipe didn't get more than two hours of sleep within a twenty-four-hour period, if he was lucky. One of the worst tests involved immobilized aquatic suffocation, or waterboarding. Other tests included offensive driving techniques, surveillance, and counter-surveillance.

Phillipe even got a rare opportunity to operate with the Sayeret Matkal. He actually got to participate in a few raids and learn something called Krav Maga, which were the most brutal hand-to-hand techniques on the planet. Talia Shia was his instructor. She was beautiful and ruthless. All training was full contact, and she kicked Phillipe's ass every single day. The funny thing, Phillipe thought, was that he had never fought girls until the military, and they took great pleasure in fucking him up.

When Phillipe awakened, his watch said three o'clock. He stuffed his money into his front pockets and retrieved his passport from the front desk. His meet was at four in a cafe a few blocks away. In Beirut, a few blocks was more dangerous than the Marcy or Jordan Downs projects on a Saturday night combined, and Phillipe had no weapons. He walked outside, and merchants came running again. But before they got to pitch their merchandise, Phillipe found a cab.

The cabby tried to speak French, and it was horrible, so Phillipe started speaking English. The cabby took that as a sign to discuss American pop culture. Fortunately, Phillipe's destination came quickly, and he tipped the cabby handsomely.

Speaking French, the hostess welcomed him to Cafe Louise. Phillipe was hungry and ordered Moules à la creme Normande with white wine. After dinner, he had coffee. Several jets passed overhead when antiaircraft fire hit an adjacent building.

While everyone scrambled for safety, an Indian man came into the restaurant and stood by Phillipe. Speaking English with a thick accent, he said, "My God, when will this activity end?"

Phillipe recognized the code and replied, "Yeah, it's a major problem. Do you have transport?"

Once the Indian man acknowledged Phillipe, the two made their way outside, where a crowd was gathering to see the extent of the damage to the building. After a short hike, they came to the Indian man's cab, which was parked in an alley. Phillipe grabbed the man and slammed him against a concrete wall and bounced his head on the ground. When the Indian man awoke, he was sitting in the backseat of the cab with a small cut on his head and Phillipe was checking his small 9mm Beretta.

Phillipe pointed the weapon and said, "What's your name?"

"Jihan," the man replied while holding his head. "My friend, why must you hit me? The major sent me."

"I never go down alleys with armed men. Besides, I don't know you, so get your ass behind the wheel and drive to the meet."

Patricia Rainbird's happiness for her parents was beyond compare. Their rekindled love bucked the trend of antagonistic post-relationships between black couples and foolish egos blinding the opportunity to correct the problems of the past. The family and church volunteers had done a magnificent job, on short notice, in preparing the ceremony.

The last time Mary and William were married, city hall was the venue. They did not have a honeymoon to speak of because Mary was already pregnant and finances were tight. This time around, William would do things the right way and treat his beautiful bride to a two-week vacation in Hawaii, a place neither had ever been.

Mary's white gown flowed down the aisle gracefully, and William stood majestically in a gray tuxedo, but both were breathless with anticipation about what the future held. Patricia relished the chance to be the maid of honor, and Goya

Rainbird made his first appearance in Los Angeles as the best man, which he was proud to do.

Before the ceremony, Goya said a few words: "I want to thank my son and his lovely bride for honoring me with this opportunity as best man. I also want to thank God for allowing me to live long enough to be here. My only concern is that Phillipe is not with us, but I have no doubt that God will return him safely to his family. Enough said. Let's get married. I'm hungry."

Before the cab stopped at a bombed-out house on a hillside, Phillipe and Jihan went through at least five checkpoints. Any asshole with a gun could set up a checkpoint. Extortion was the main purpose of the checkpoint, not safety. Everyone was forced to pay or denied access. If anyone caused a problem, they were shot. Luckily, Jihan was known and wasn't charged as much.

The neighborhood where the meet was being held was controlled by the Druze, basically the niggas of the Muslim world because of their pluralism philosophy. Both the Shi'a and Sunni hated the Druze and had been trying to exterminate them for centuries.

Phillipe made Jihan walk in front of him. Night had fallen and covered everything in darkness. They entered into what looked like a vestibule. The burned-out structure reeked of mildew, and the squeaky floors made a silent approach impossible. A voice in the distance calmly said, "Rainbird. What the fuck?"

The major appeared from the darkness. "Put the gun down."

Phillipe complied. All at once, two other figures emerged from their hiding positions. One person Phillipe recognized said, "Hey, young buck, have you learned anything yet?" It was Master Chief Tomlinson.

Phillipe said, "We'll see," and they shook hands. The other person was another guy with long brown hair.

The major told Jihan to wait in the car and keep a lookout. Phillipe returned his firearm to him without the clip or round chambered. The major turned and introduced Gunnery Sergeant David McManus, USMC, Force Recon, Scout-Sniper. They nodded to one another but kept their distance.

The major informed Phillipe and Gunny that they would be partners, which was an unwelcome surprise to both. The plan was to cause as much havoc as possible to the Hezbollah and Iranian Republican Guard operations in the Beqaa Valley and elsewhere. This last point was of particular interest to Phillipe. When asked to elaborate, the major surprisingly uttered, "We hunt the fuckers, and we catch or kill them, whichever is convenient. Oh, by the way, you have a lot of mail, Rainbird. You got five."

Phillipe found a place to sit down and opened his mail. Using a small flashlight, he skimmed through it quickly until he came upon a letter from his father saying he was marrying Mary today.

When the guests of the William and Mary Rainbird wedding arrived at the Proud Bird banquet hall, they saw the beautiful floral arrangements of red and white carnations. The DJ's sound system pumped out new and old school R and B, funk, and disco. The catered food was from Roscoe's House of Chicken and Waffles. An ice sculpture of a flower sat alongside the champagne fountain, but nothing could compare with the fellowship between the guests of family and friends, old and young.

Patricia's joy had overwhelmed her all day. She wished her brother could have experienced this day and seen the positive outcome of heartache. She knew better than most how her brother had changed from a fun-loving bookworm to someone with a notorious reputation for hurting people. The neighborhood stories were numerous, but one really upset her down to her bones.

When Phillipe was twelve, one of his classmates had bullied him for an entire school year, but he had never retaliated. When Patricia heard about this, she questioned his strange behavior. Phillipe told Pat not to worry about it, which made her worry even more. Pat knew her brother was a schemer, and he wouldn't take shit for very long. One month before summer vacation, Patricia heard that a boy broke his back during gym class and had be rushed to the hospital. When she found out that it was the same boy who was messing with Phillipe, she knew what happened. Patricia asked Phillipe for an explanation, and he said don't worry about it.

Patricia just wanted Phillipe to have peace of mind and be happy, especially since all of his friends were at the reception eating, drinking, and dancing. His last two girlfriends, Michele and Jennifer, the Landon family, even Uncle (don't call him uncle) Jack were looking as if they were enjoying themselves. Two of Phillipe's friends, whom Pat had never met, said they would like to pay respects to the bride and groom. They had a very large present with flowers, and she said of course. She asked their names, and they replied Rufus and Sonny. Not knowing any better, she walked over to the bridal table and started to make introductions.

Jennifer Parker saw what was going on. She came between the newlyweds and politely asked, "So, who do we have here?"

Pat: "Oh, this is Rufus and Sonny. They are Phillipe's friends."

Rufus: "I'm just paying my respects with a little gift."

Jenn: "I'll take it to the gift room."

Rufus: "I know you. You're the Crowbar's daughter. The word is he don't like niggas. Here you are at a nigga wedding."

William: "Look, neither my wife nor I know you, so I suggest you leave, brother."

Sonny: "Time to go."

Rufus looked over his shoulder and saw that ten to twelve men, including a big Indian man, were surrounding them. Knowing when to leave the party, he said, "I'm sorry, sir. I didn't mean to disrespect anyone. I wish y'all nothing but happiness."

He turned toward the exit and swiftly left. Sonny was watching his back, particularly the big Indian fellow, who had a look on his face that was indescribable. A car was waiting by the curb. Rufus turned to the crowd and said, "Tell Phillipe to come talk to me when he gets out."

Sonny opened the rear door, and Rufus got in. So did Sonny, and the car drove away.

Mary wanted to know who the hell was that and how in the world did her son know a thug named Rufus. William asked Jack what was going on, and Jack told him as much as he knew and promised to protect the family from harm. But he never spoke of Phillipe's criminal activities.

William didn't buy all of it, but he had something to tell Mary. He felt that at some point this would sort itself out. In the gift room, Sammy Landon and Jennifer carefully opened the present Rufus had brought. What they saw scared the shit out of both of them. The box held a WP grenade. Jennifer said, "After the reception, there's a meeting in my room at midnight."

September twenty-second, 1982, 8:22 a.m., Bonn, Federal Republic of Germany. The early fall rain hung over the city as evidence that the seasonal change to autumn would not go unnoticed. Helen Masters' morning commute with thousands of other people formed the human traffic flow into the public rail stations. Helen walked the wet Bavarian streets to the British embassy. She could have driven or received transport, but she was doing more than just exercise. She was trying to clear her head and get rid of the headache that was created by a hangover.

The Falklands War had ended as abruptly as it had begun, with the Argentinean government choosing to surrender after only a couple thousand casualties and over ten thousand POWs. When Helen returned from the Falklands, she started to party and drink heavily, like most veterans. Post-stress disorders manifested themselves in civilian or noncombat situations, and the symptoms were unique to the individual.

MI6 had a rising star in Helen Masters and wanted to make sure that the process of creating an elite field operative had not taken its toll. Helen, for her part, was happy to get back into the field. Her Nana was recovering nicely and had started walking with a cane. Nana's speech was a little awkward, but that had improved since Helen had been away, and father Reilly's daily visits were always a pleasure.

But, no matter how good everything was, Helen's restlessness kept her up at night, and that lead to the partying. Her brisk two-mile morning walk burned off the residual effects. Most people rested or drank more alcohol to recover from a hangover, which could not be farther from the true remedy. The body is a biological furnace, and when a foreign substance is ingested, the body will accept or reject it. So, increasing one's metabolism increases the body's ability to reject alcohol quickly and naturally.

Helen made her way through several security checkpoints, and, feeling better, she greeted everyone good morning with her usual smile. The British embassy in Bonn was in a perfect location—far enough away from Eastern Europe not to feel like a prison camp and close enough to Paris for a weekend shopping trip. As soon as Helen exited the lift on the third floor, she was met by Margaret Wade, the secretary for Helen's superior, Mr. Addison, and told she was wanted immediately. Helen walked directly to the office of Bryan Addison and knocked firmly. Upon entering, she noticed a distinguished gentleman standing to meet her.

Mr. Addison: "Good morning, Helen. I would like you to meet Sean Davis. He runs all of our ops in West Berlin."

Mr. Davis: "It's so nice to make your acquaintance. I have heard so many wonderful things about you."

Helen: "It's my pleasure. I've heard a lot about you. You spoke at a seminar at Fort Monckton."

Mr. Davis: "Really? Well, I hope it helped."

Helen: "Every bit does."

Mr. Addison: "We asked you here today to learn if you're ready for field work."

Helen: "Yes, sir."

Mr. Davis: "Before you say yes, let's be clear. Female operatives have to be willing to do whatever is necessary to accomplish the mission, including seduction."

Helen: "I understand, sir."

"Mr. Addison: "All right. Pack your things. You're going to Berlin."

When Detective Adam Canaby got word of a complaint at the Rainbird wedding, he thought the pieces were coming together. Rufus Jackson had just fucked up, and now Canaby could investigate Phillipe Rainbird without raising suspicion. The original investigators were more than happy to turn over the case. In their opinion, it was dog shit and would only interfere with their social agendas at the strip club.

Canaby rang the doorbell of the Rainbird family. A male voice said, "Can I help you?"

Canaby and Barnes introduced themselves while presenting their credentials. The large black iron door opened, and Willie Rainbird invited the two detectives inside. Mary Rainbird was sitting in the living room with two other women. The detectives continued the introductions, and to the detectives' surprise, the Rainbirds had invited their lawyer, Katherine McKay. Also present was Michele Matthews.

Canaby hadn't expected this. His aggressive strategy needed to change, but no matter what, he was going to get some answers.

Canaby: "I will try to wrap this up as quickly as possible. I read the preliminary and original investigators' reports. That being said, I have some follow-up questions. Has anyone seen Mr. Jackson in the area?"

Willie: "No. We told our neighbors about the restraining order that was issued."

Mrs. McKay: "I served the order through my office, and it's confirmed. He was served."

Canaby: "Does anyone know why Mr. Jackson is so interested in Phillipe?"

Mary: "Isn't that your job?"

Canaby: "Well, ma'am, my theory is that Phillipe, at some point in time, was involved in some sort of criminal activity."

Willie: "That may be true at some point, but now my son is at this very moment risking his life for this country. And as long as that's the case, you will refrain from insulting my family. Have I made myself clear?"

Canaby: "I apologize. May I continue?"

Barnes: "Sir, may I use the bathroom, please?"

Willie: "Sure. Follow me."

Willie escorted detective Barnes to the bathroom and returned to the meeting. Barnes went inside, closing the door behind him. He waited a few moments, then quietly opened the door. There were three bedrooms. The large one was obviously occupied by the parents. The door of one was closed, and the other had pictures of Willie Mays hanging on the wall. That had to be it, Barnes thought, moving swiftly to the closet and opening it to find what he was looking for.

Willie Rainbird's paranoia had started to eat away at his attention to the conversation. He got up to see why the hell Barnes was taking so long. Just before getting to the bathroom door, he heard a loud flushing of water. When Barnes opened the door, a repugnant odor followed.

Willie said, "Goddamn it, man, spray some of that Lysol."

Barnes's excuse was he wasn't feeling well and he should probably leave.

Canaby finished his interview, made his apologies for his partner, and left, leaving the Rainbird family with an unsatisfied taxpayer feeling.

After a block or so, Canaby asked, "Did you get something?"

Barnes pulled out an old pair of Nike jogging shoes and said, "We got it."

September twenty-fifth, 1982, 12:00 a.m., southeast Los Angeles, California. Big Trace Strong and Huey sat in a car on 117th street and Wadsworth, which was a vacant lot, though not because of a lack of urban development. The state had bought up all the houses over a decade ago. The powers that be claimed that they would build a freeway, but like most things in the ghetto, it was just another broken promise.

Big and Huey were waiting for this country nigga, Nahlense, to bring a gift-wrapped present. Apparently, Speedy wanted to turn Big out like a hoe, and Nahlense, in his zeal to hook up Big with this information, showed his natural black ass. Big knew Speedy wasn't smart or strong enough to come after Big unless Nahlense sent out signals. So, to prove his loyalty, Nahlense would pop a cap into Speedy's punk ass. But Nahlense didn't know that as soon as he pulled the trigger, he was a dead muthafucka. A car turned the corner and flashed its headlights. The driver was Speedy. He got out, followed by Nahlense and Sonny.

Speedy walked over to Big to shake hands, and Huey punched him in the jaw. Nahlense pulled out a nickel-plated .45. Speedy said, "Hey, man, what you doing?"

Nahlense: "Sorry, baby, but you a backstabbing bitch."

Nahlense shot three times into the face of Speedy, and Huey pointed his Smith and Wesson .357 at Nahlense's head. Sonny started to beg for his life. Not showing any mercy, Big slapped Sonny across the face and told him to shut the fuck up. Walking over to Nahlense, he whispered, "Country ass boy, this is LA. Kill this nigga!"

Huey cocked the pistol and, at the last instant, shot Big in the stomach. Nahlense picked up his .45 and smiled while saying," No shit, nigga. What happened? Did your best man just shoot yo ass? You know what? You right. This is LA."

All three unloaded their weapons into Big's body.

September twenty-sixth, 1982, 3:00 a.m., Beqaatet Aachquot, Lebanon. Phillipe Rainbird lay in the bushes near a road used by Hezbollah to bring weapons into Beirut. The real-time intelligence that he had gathered indicated a large shipment would pass through this location. He was at the forefront of Operation Fire Cat, a black bag op to conduct black operations against all Iranian forces in and around the Lebanese area of operations, or AO. The unit was small but had priority with normal units. All information concerning Fire Cat was above top secret. Iranians used these dirt roads at night, which meant they had some form of night vision. This was an advantage the unit would exploit. The kill box was set with claymore mines. Major Corran's job was to destroy the escort vehicle with an RPG-7.

Master Chief and McManus had overwatch with sniper rifles. The comms broke squelch, and the Major said, "Two trucks, no lights, about three clicks. Stand to gentlemen."

After several distance updates, the major indicated that the first truck was the target, which meant do not destroy and, if possible, take prisoners.

Phillipe prepared himself to take the truck cleanly. Both trucks rolled slowly into the kill box. Master Chief started a countdown: five, four, three, two, one. First, Mac shot both drivers, and Master Chief blew the claymore. This caused the truck to jackknife while skidding to a stop. That's when the major fired the RPG-7 into the cargo area. Mac surgically picked off the stragglers. Phillipe jumped into the driver's seat of the target truck and pistol-whipped the passenger. He stopped the truck before it ran off the road.

Phillipe was about to cuff the passenger when he saw in the side-view mirror an asshole with an AK-47 running toward the cab. When a bullet hit the guy in the side of the head, Phillipe's comms squelched, and Mac said, "You're welcome, Mr. Pelican."

Helen Masters awoke in a West Berlin hotel and took a groggy stroll to the bathroom. En route, she noticed two sets of clothing. She turned to see her new boss, Sean Davis, naked in the sack.

"Shite" was the one answer that seemed to fix the moment. Besides drinking, she had become somewhat neurotic in her sexual aggressiveness after her last failed relationship. She always took responsibility for her behavior and never felt victimized, but this was different. She was finally moving up the operational ladder. Women in the workplace had to overcome stereotypes and lower pay, and she didn't want her colleagues to think she slept her way through life.

When she returned from the bathroom, Mr. Davis was sitting up and smiling at her. He said, "Good morning, Ms. Masters. Slept well?"

Helen: "Well enough, thank you. Listen, this can't go on. Not that it wasn't nice, but it's inappropriate."

Davis: "I agree."

Helen: "So no hard feelings?"

Davis: "Of course not. We're professionals. Sentiment

is not part of our nature. Now that that's over, let's get down to work. Your assignment starts now. Here's your brief. Do your homework and destroy the brief in the manner instructed. All necessary equipment and logistics will be provided. You may not make contact with headquarters. Understood?"

Helen: "Yes, sir."

Davis: "Oh, by the way, you've been promoted to captain."

Helen told him thank you and began reading the file. Her eagerness skyrocketed. The target name was Amir Lebeau.

Phillipe Rainbird moved into a defensive position to stand his security watch. Being the junior member of the unit, he had all the shit jobs. But this was better than driving a cab all day though the streets of Beirut, which can only be described as driving in Tijuana on acid. Customers would enter the cab and talk in their native language, and Phillipe would pretend not to understand. Sometimes during the cross talk, pieces of a conversation had usable intel. Actually, Phillipe needed some time to himself to sort out his burgeoning problems back home. He had been in contact with Jenn, and she told him what happened at the wedding. Most of the info she had was from the streets and wasn't very reliable, but he had a name—Rufus muthafuckin' Jackson from New Orleans.

His main boy was some punk named Sonny Otis, and Jack was down there watching them. Phillipe knew he was not in a position of strength to deal with this clown. He needed leverage against Mr. Jackson's crew, and being twelve thousand miles away protected everyone, because Phillipe wasn't a threat.

As soon as Phillipe appeared and declined to work for Mr. Jackson's crew, there would be a war. Mac's voice came through the earpiece indicating that Phillipe was being relieved and wanted back at the safe house.

Phillipe walked in, and Master Chief was securing a badly beaten prisoner. The major motioned to the back room. The major closed the door, and they both sat down.

T.C.: "What I'm about to tell you is classified. About ten years ago, the KGB and the CIA had major purges within their respective organizations. Everyone was selling secrets to everyone for one thing—profit. Because they all knew each other, when one would get caught spying, the others would assist with transportation, papers, and money. They started a corporation that has infiltrated every aspect of business, including the black market. They call themselves IZMENENIYE, or the change. Our friend told us that the change was going to provide Iran and Iraq with a nuclear ballistic missile. Allegedly, their goal is to change the balance of power in the Middle East."

Phillipe: "Hold the fuck up. Are you saying that an international criminal organization is trying to dominate the world?"

T.C.: "Financially, yes."

Phillipe: "So, does the leader of this organization have a muthafuckin' cat?"

Master Chief: "Hey! This is serious shit. If we don't stop them, there will be nuclear war.

T.C.: "And if we do, not only are we in danger, but our families are. These cocksuckers don't leave loose ends."

Master Chief: "But we have one advantage. Our unit is off the books if we do it right."

T.C.: "OK, I vote yes."

Master Chief: "Yes. I speak for Mac too."

Phillipe: "Yes, on one condition. Can I be the one to drop the bald-headed leader into the smokestack?"

Canaby and Barnes looked on as the forensics team worked the crime scene of the late Big Trace Armstrong and Speedy Randell Green. So far, the wallets found in the pockets of the victims were the only way to identify the bodies. Twenty-two bullets were fired into Big, ten to the head. The point was made. The problem was, everyone knew who the perpetrators were. But with no eyewitnesses or murder weapons, Canaby was powerless. Sure, Canaby could bring in Nahlense and Sonny for a little sweat session, but these assholes would just lawyer up. They knew the game better than most cops, and even if Canaby let the goon squad give them a four-wall conference, the time wasted could be better spent at just waiting for Nahlense to make a mistake.

Criminals always made errors in judgment, like Phillipe Rainbird. After the detectives had left the Rainbird home, they went to Venice Beach. Before visiting the Douglas residence, the detectives circled the block to see how much damage had been repaired. To their surprise, the lot where the gas house murders had taken place was empty. All debris had been removed. But one could see right into the backyard of Mr. and Mrs. Douglas.

When Canaby called the Douglases, there was no answer. But he didn't need their presence. Besides, it was probably for the best.

Canaby approached the main gate, and before he got within five feet, the doberman gang hit the fence in a ferocious manner. The barking increased with every step until he got close enough to the gate to pull out Phillipe's old jogging shoe. One sniff, and the dobermans' behavior become less hostile. The female dog started to lick the shoe. The male dog's pink penis became erect.

Barnes, observing in disbelief, uttered, "Fuck me."

Canaby felt vindicated but knew that canine testimony was inadmissible in a court of law. Now, he had bigger fish to fry. There was a drug war on the horizon, and nobody was coming out unscathed.

 # Chapter 9

October eleventh, 1982, 10:00 a.m., somewhere in northern New Mexico. Apache Jack was riding hard and fast through the mountainous terrain taking a path only he knew. Jack's mind was focused and determined. He got to a point where the road, such as it was, ended, and he turned the jeep around and parked. He got out and started the two-mile hike up a steep hill.

Once on top, there was a valley. In reality, it was a dormant volcano. There he saw a man with long dark hair doing chores. Jack made sure everything looked normal before descending.

He walked slowly into the camp area. The long-haired man said, "I see you. I heard your jeep come up the mountain. You hungry?"

The man looked up at Jack, and Jack nodded before saying, "We have work for you. Are you ready?"

The man said, "Of course." He handed Jack a plate and asked, "Who and how many?"

Jack's eyes narrowed to emphasize his point. "Whoever and as many as it takes, Dracula."

The Fête des Vendanges, or the Montmartre Grape Harvest, was located in a northern Paris community sitting on top of a hill. The festival was lively, and people were friendly. This was not a place one would think an international smuggler would enjoy, but Amir Lebeau loved being there.

Amir had grown up in Clichy-sous-Bois, the French version of the projects. His parents were poor Nigerian immigrants. Jobs and opportunities were hard to come by, so he took to the streets, stealing and selling drugs. When he became old enough, he joined the French army for six years and was able to move his family into a decent apartment. He got a job as an enforcer for the local crime lord until he fell off a building. As luck would have it, Amir took over.

Amir watched the parade with his best friend, Louis, and drank wine. Amir was an international playboy and preferred blondes, which was why he couldn't stop staring at a woman standing across the street. He smiled and waved. The buxom woman waved back.

Amir accepted the initiative and walked over. Their conversation varied between the festival and the personal. She said her name was Lucy Mae Stratton from Houston, Texas, and this was her first time in Europe. Amir thought she was quaint, so he invited her to dinner. That evening was filled with modified stories of Amir's travels. Amir became very interested in Lucy's stories about her rich father who didn't understand her. He pressed the issue and discovered that Daddy was the CEO of Stratton Oil. They were huge in Nigeria, and Amir realized this young girl was his ticket out of the life. So he worked his magic with promises of fun and adventure. Everything would be red carpets, private jets, and five-star hotels.

The thought made Lucy excited with anticipation. Amir didn't want to move too fast, so he escorted Lucy back to her room and softly kissed her on the hand. Before saying good night, they agreed to meet for breakfast and spend the day together. Lucy closed her door. She locked it and looked through the peephole to make sure he'd left. She went to the toilettes and removed the blonde wig.

Helen was so relieved the night was over. Amir was not an attractive man, which made this job twice as hard. She had to pretend he was someone else just to laugh at his stupid jokes, and the only person she could come up with was Mr. Rainbird. While soaking in a hot bath and drinking wine, she tried to rationalize by thinking about a man she'd briefly met once. The obvious thing was race. They were both black, so it was a natural point of reference, and Helen stopped trying to deny she was attracted Mr. Rainbird. She started to calculate how long it would take to get close to the objective. Her mind was becoming cloudy, and soon she was asleep.

October fifteenth, 1982, 9:00 p.m., USS Grayback (SSG-574), Mediterranean Sea, Lat: 36.085, Long: 32.267. This was Phillipe's first real experience operating from a submarine. The Grayback was the last diesel submarine in the United States arsenal that wasn't a museum. In true naval benevolence, the Grayback was the only sub configured for what the Navy called troop movement. Phillipe guessed that was how the Pentagon referred to Navy SEALs. The official policy was not to acknowledge the existence of SEALs. The reasoning was maybe operational security, but everyone in Washington, D.C., knew. Which meant everyone in the Kremlin knew. Besides, the Green Berets' existence was not a secret, especially since John fuckin' Wayne had made a major motion picture about their experiences in Vietnam.

Master Chief had told Phillipe the Navy didn't want a bunch of recruits trying to be SEALs, and somebody had to work the mess decks. Mr. Pelican should know that better than anyone. Master Chief had taken it upon himself to be

Phillipe's sea daddy, or mentor. The only thing Phillipe was getting a tired of was his shit. But that was the point. Phillipe was learning that discretion and tact should be in his social toolbox.

Master Chief debriefed the attending six members of SEAL Team Three. He included finding out IZMENENIYE involvement and that the Iranian prisoner was an intelligence officer, or IO. The major had persuaded the IO to divulge the location of a high-level meeting on a Panamanian cargo ship named the SS Memento de Cambio. Phillipe spoke fluid Spanish and thought it was too much of a coincidence that the target on this op was called Moment of Change. For the first time, he became afraid that he had put his family in even greater danger. But he couldn't go back and become passive. The only way to solve the problem was to attack it.

The SS Memento dropped anchor about five nautical miles south of Grayback's position. The ISA unit of Phillipe and Mac entered the starboard lockout chamber. Mac felt compelled to inform Phillipe that a few months ago, this same chamber had malfunctioned and six SEALs had died. Phillipe's response was crude but appropriate. "Suck my dick."

Mac laughed while he checked his gear and prepared to exit the sub. There was a loud hissing sound followed by water flooding the chamber. Once flooded, the pressure equalized so Phillipe could open the escape hatch. As he exited, he saw the SEAL Delivery Vehicle Team, or SDVT, launching a wet submersible with SEAL Team Three assisting. After SDV separated from the Grayback, the SDVT members signaled everyone aboard. Phillipe entered the cramped driver bay and immediately transferred to the SDV oxygen system. Now, the rule was you were not supposed to go to sleep, but sitting in complete darkness with the hum of the lithium ion-powered motor, which acted as a lullaby. So Phillipe just rested his eyes one at a time.

A few hours later, eight divers swam through the murky Mediterranean water. Mac was team leader, and Phillipe's luminous navigation equipment led the way. SEAL Team Three's job was to mine the Memento at the keel and provide exfiltration support. The ISA unit had to search the ship for intel.

Phillipe and Mac were swim buddies, tied together by a cable until they got to the Memento. After undonning their scuba gear, Phillipe and Mac infiltrated the ship, port and starboard respectively. Mac's job was to search the ship below the weather deck. He entered an open aft hatch and found an empty compartment to set up comms. Phillipe's job was to search from the weather deck to the bridge. But first he had to evade the aft watch. This was a reconn mission, engagement only if necessary.

While the sentry made his rounds, Phillipe kept to the shadows of the aft capsian and other loading equipment. He took a moment to get his comms up. He heard Mac's voice saying, "Red actual, this Red one."

Red actual: "We got you Red one, five by five."

Red one: "Red two, you up?"

Phillipe: "Yeah, I'm here."

Red one: "I'm starting my search. Report status every ten minutes. Keep comms clear. Copy?"

Red two: "Copy."

Phillipe saw his chance to move into the main

passageway and up to 01 level. Mac moved silently though the berthing area, which smelled of sweat and feet. He came to an area that had two guards watching a large hatch to the cargo bay. Strange, Mac thought. He couldn't go through without notice, so he had to find the escape hatch.

The comms squelched: "Red team be advised of small craft approaching your locale. Copy?"

Phillipe: "Copy. I got eyes on. Four tangos with AK-47s. Four principals carrying two silver cases. Copy?"

Red actual: "Roger that."

Phillipe was lying down on a maintenance catwalk above, observing the meet and greet. The entourage made its way to the captain's quarters, and the security team broke up into stations—one guarding the outer passageway, one guarding port and starboard of the cabin, and one guarding the small craft.

When SEAL Team Three saw the small craft, they automatically placed mines to destroy it. Phillipe quietly moved above the starboard side, where he found a portal to the cabin. He reached into his watertight knapsack and retrieved a twelve-inch black tube. This was a fiber optic camera with a telescoping lens shaft. It was a high-tech version of a kid's toy that came in cereal boxes.

Once in position, Phillipe took several pictures of all the participants, who included three white men, two Persians, and one black man. When Phillipe took a harder look, he knew he recognized the black man. He'd met him at a party through Husam. Phillipe's alias was that he worked for Husam running munitions into Beirut. This gave Phillipe access to Husam's boss, Amir, who was very flashy with his money and mouth. Amir liked to gamble, and Phillipe won a $15,000-dollar pot playing poker. After losing, Amir didn't have shit to say. Husam was very worried that Amir would kill his friend. Phillipe, or Andre, had to promise a rematch.

The cabin door guard entered and took the silver cases to the bridge. Phillipe wanted a look inside those cases, so he secured his camera. The guard below was smoking a cigarette and not paying attention. Phillipe climbed down silently and pulled out his Fairbairn Sykes knife. In one swift move, he grabbed the guard's forehead and slid the knife into the base of his skull with a twist. The guard's body stiffened and relaxed without a sound. He was dead. Phillipe laid the body down and began to pick the locks on the silver cases.

The first case was filled with money, hundred-dollar denominations, American. So was the second case, but it also had financial documents, some in French and the others in German. Without hesitation, Phillipe filled his diver's ditty bag with the money and put the documents in his knapsack.

In the meantime, Mac heard some interesting cross talk between the guys guarding the large crate. They spoke French and shared that they both were concerned about radiation poisoning. Mac told Red actual he was going in hot and pulled out his Smith and Wesson model 39 with a suppressor.

Two heads shots later, Mac was opening the crate to find something that looked like an old refrigerator. He took some pictures before closing the crate and attaching a beacon.

Mac: "Red actual, this is Red one. Copy?"

"I got you, Red one. I found fat boy. Repeat, I found fat boy. Copy?"

"Roger that. Fat boy in pocket. Red two, you copy?"

"I copy. I'm gonna need to change to backup RV. Copy?"

"Roger that. You need assist on your exfil?"

"Negative. Can't stay on unsecured comms. Backup RV."

"Red team backup RV is a go. Have a nice day."

Mac made his way back to the escape hatch and up to the weather deck and silently entered the water.

Phillipe finished packing the money. He booby-trapped the cases with IEDs, and he packed up. Just before he jumped over the side of the ship, the guard walked in. Phillipe had no choice but to shoot him twice. He then jumped overboard. The ship alarms started to blare, and the sentries fired aimlessly into the water. The leader of the entourage took a look inside one of the cases, and two large explosions engulfed the confined space. The strength of Phillipe's swimming was put to the test because, as the money absorbed the seawater, it became exponentially heavier. The only reason he didn't drown was two members of SEAL Team Three grabbed the bag and attached an inflatable buoy to it. They also had Phillipe's scuba, which he re-donned immediately.

The backup RV was three miles east of the Memento, a trawler flying a Greek flag that was manned by the major and Talia. Before Phillipe was fished out of the sea, Mac was screaming at him for fuckin' the op and giving orders to change the RV.

Phillipe calmly said, "Mac, if you look in that ditty bag, you will have all the answers."

The major opened the sack and said, "Holy shit! You

got this from the ship?"

Phillipe: "Yes, sir. As you see, I could not take all that money back to the sub, and I have documents."

Mac: "What are we going to do?"

Phillipe: "Keep it."

Just then, the Memento de Cambio broke in half and lifted out of the water. With dozens of secondary explosions, the ship slowly sank. The major recognized that his guys needed leadership and said, "All right, the fireworks show is over. Talia, set a course for Cypress. Pelican, you wash, Mac you dry, and I'll go over these documents."

A well-known associate of Nahlense Rufus Jackson sat in a French Quarter bar doing shots. He needed to piss and staggered to the restroom. While being bumped, he felt a sting on the back of his neck. Once he got to the restroom, his stomach started to turn and he felt a sharp pain in his chest. He fell in the stall and tried to call for help until he died.

Across the street at a phone booth, a man dressed in black made a call. After several rings, a female voice answered. The man said, 'Yeah, this is Dracula. One down."

He hung up and disappeared. Jennifer hung up thinking, "It has begun."

October twenty-second, 7:00 p.m., Monte-Carlo, Monaco. The Grand Casino's spacious vestibule was luxury at its finest. From the plush carpeting to the opulent crystal chandeliers and the service, it was beyond five stars. The ISA team's presence there had a twofold mission. First, to deposit $10 million dollars that had been confiscated on the last mission. Also, the actionable intel of the financial documents suggested that Amir Lebeau was the next rung on the ladder.

Phillipe used Husam to contact Amir about another poker game. Amir invited Phillipe, or Andre, to his Monaco estate. Before she left, Talia got eyes on the mansion. She had to get back because she was on point to find the other nuclear device before it got into the hands of Saddam Hussein. The United States Navy had recovered the other bomb at the bottom of the sea. Because the core had corroded, it was leaking radiation and was unstable. The United States Navy EOD lived up to their reputation and secured the device enough for transportation.

Phillipe had been playing blackjack for the last hour and winning handsomely. A beautiful blonde woman looked on with approval, so Phillipe bought her some champagne and struck up a whimsical conversation.

Amir's entourage came into the casino, and all of the concierges surrounded him to make sure his needs were satisfied. When Phillipe and Amir's eyes met, they both smiled like sharks with a casual head gesture. Phillipe got a look at the white girl Amir was with, and she seemed familiar. His second glance must have been telepathic because she looked him square in the eye.

Phillipe's grandfather Goya had always said he had good instincts. But this time, Phillipe hoped he was wrong. Those weren't the eyes of a stranger, but she looked so different, he had to be sure. Phillipe's new friend, Inga, was becoming more impressed with his gambling skill and wondered out loud what else the young man could be good at. Phillipe told Inga he had an important meeting to attend and he would like to make an appointment to give her an erotic demonstration. They made plans for Monday evening and said good night.

Amir was trying his hand at baccarat and not doing very well, from what Phillipe had witnessed, but he has more concerned with Amir's date. She was wearing an elegant dress, and her familiar cleavage filled it out. Phillipe knew without a doubt that Lieutenant Masters was wearing a wig. He stood at the bar staring at her, and she glanced up several times before whispering something into Amir's ear. He waved her away because he was losing, and she walked slowly over to the bar.

She ordered a drink in a thick hillbilly accent that made Phillipe chuckle. Phillipe introduced himself as Andre Gacon, and she said her name was Lucy Mae Stratton. Phillipe almost bit a hole in his lip trying not to laugh. She seemed a little pissed off and said farewell. Phillipe noticed she'd left a matchbook. He turned, finished his drink, palmed the book of matches, went to the men's room, and entered a stall. He opened the book. The handwriting said Hotel de Monte-Carlo, room 313, one hour.

Fifty-five minutes later, Phillipe strolled through the lobby of the Hotel de Monte-Carlo. Beforehand, he had checked in with Mac and Master Chief. The major had flown back to ISA headquarters in Fort Belvoir, Virginia, for a little face-to-face with the CO, code name Pinnacle. Phillipe was not high enough on the food chain to know Pinnacle's real name or rank.

The elevator doors opened at the third floor, and

Phillipe walked to the door marked 313. He knocked three times while listening for footsteps. Helen opened the door and invited Phillipe in, still using the hillbilly accent. Before Phillipe could react, she pulled out a Walther PPK.

Helen: "Don't move. Are you armed?"

Phillipe: "Yes."

Helen: "With your left hand, remove the weapon using only two fingers."

Phillipe complied and said, "Who taught you that fuckin' accent?"

Helen: "Never mind. What are you doing here?"

Phillipe: "Well, I thought I was coming here to lay some serious pipe, but the gun is spoiling the mood."

Helen: "You make jokes, but I will kill you."

Phillipe: "I know. I'm working. What are you doing?" She lowered her weapon.

Helen: "So am I. What's your mission?"

Phillipe: "Your boyfriend. And yours?"

Helen: "His safe. He has something I want."

Phillipe: "Besides his company?"

Helen didn't dignify that last comment with a response because it sounded like jealousy, and she took the high road.

Helen: "Well enough. Once I complete my objective, you can do whatever you want."

Phillipe: "Here's the deal. We have a poker game

scheduled tonight, and 'whatever' is now.

Helen: "Bollocks."

Phillipe: "No, the dog's bollocks. We need each other, like it or not. Where's your backup?"

Helen: "I don't have any, just a contact after the job's done."

Phillipe: "Your call, Lieutenant."

Helen: "All right. Follow my lead and don't fuck up."

Phillipe: "Yes, ma'am."

The limousine carrying Phillipe drove up to the security shack in front of Amir's estate. The guard took a quick look inside and waved the car through. Phillipe's mind was busy calculating the possibilities, including the one Mac had suggested, that Helen was really a part of this and Phillipe would have to kill her. He owed her a lot, and he'd refrained from really trying to hurt her during extensive hand-to-hand sessions. But if the bitch tried any shit, he was more than willing to fuck her up really bad. That was a depressing thought because he liked her and she would be the first life he'd taken with a positive emotional connection.

The palatial estate was beautiful and well lit, which made Mac and Master Chief's job a little harder. But they were experienced professionals. Upon Phillipe's arrival, Amir greeted and searched his challenger at the door. While escorting Phillipe to the game room, Amir gave him a mini tour.

Phillipe had memorized the estate layout provided by Talia. She had done a good job; her details were down to the color of the carpets. The game room had a high-end billiards table, plush red carpet, mahogany wood paneling, and full bar, where Lucy Mae was standing sipping a martini. The game table had three basic chairs and one special chair for Amir. After some pleasantries, which included drinks, they both sat down.

Phillipe was sitting with his back to the billiards table as planned. The clock on the wall read five past midnight, which meant all hell would break loose in twenty-five minutes. Amir was a degenerate gambler, and as long as he was winning, everything was right with the world, so Phillipe let him win. After about ten minutes, Lucy Mae scurried upstairs to the safe in Amir's bedroom. She retrieved a well-hidden safe-cracking device from under a piece of furniture. First, she had to disable the electronic eye behind the picture frame. She took a piece of duct tape and a mirror from a dental instrument and maneuvered it slowly between the wall and the picture. She attached the cracking device and worked the combination.

Downstairs, Phillipe's ego got the better of him, and he started to win. Amir began cussing in French. Not knowing what to do, he ordered a drink, and while he was preoccupied, Phillipe slid his hand under the table to find the Sig Sauer P220 that Talia had placed there.

Suddenly, there were multiple screams from everywhere. Amir ordered his bodyguards to find Lucy Mae and ordered Andre to stay still. Once the bodyguards left the room, Amir pulled out a chrome-plated Smith and Wesson .38 Special. Amir thought the police were coming and began to panic. He was turning to seek Andre's consul when he noticed that there was a gun on him.

Phillipe: "Put the gun down, and you live."

Amir yelled, "No!" and tried to shoot Phillipe. But he caught two in the chest and one in the head before he hit the floor.

Phillipe jumped to his feet and ran toward Helen. Before getting there, he encountered one bodyguard trying to reload his weapon. Phillipe ran through him like Jack Tatum. When Phillipe finally got to Helen's location, he found two bodyguards dead on the floor.

Phillipe: "I guess you don't need help."

Helen: "Apparently not. Thanks for sharing your invasion plans."

Phillipe: "Loose lips, Lieutenant. You got what you needed, so the rest is mine."

Helen: "Have at it. Oh, by the way, it's Captain now."

Helen pranced victoriously out of the bedroom because she had completed her assignment and had gotten in the last word, which was so important for women.

Phillipe was relieved that she was unharmed. He collected the other documents and proceeded downstairs. Mac and Master Chief were introducing themselves to the lovely British agent. Helen said her good-byes and borrowed one of Amir's black Mercedeses. Master Chief tried to convince Helen that backup would be advisable, but that didn't give her pause. She had already made arrangements with her contact, and she was leaving the country tonight. The black Mercedes Benz sped away.

Master Chief saw Phillipe's worried look and said, "Damn, boy. You got it bad. Follow that woman before I have to hurt you. We'll stay here and torch the place."

Mac and Master Chief had a field day teasing Phillipe about his crush on the captain while they setting fire to the mansion with incinerator grenades. Phillipe found the keys to a BMW 320i and chased Helen to a luxurious apartment complex. While parking, Phillipe saw Helen walk through a security door. He ran across the street, got a look at the lock, and pulled out the appropriate tool from the kit. Within fifteen seconds, the gate opened.

He casually walked to the elevator and saw it was stopping on the fourth floor. He took the stairs rapidly. When he opened the fourth-floor stairwell door, he heard a crash. Phillipe listened carefully. When he got to room 407, the commotion got louder. The doorjamb was broken. He peeked in to see a tall, pale man fighting with Helen.

Phillipe charged in with no regard for his own safety and threw the tall man's ass out the window. The man hit a closed dumpster, which made him bounce in the air and land hard. The fall didn't kill him, and Phillipe was determined to finish the job before he noticed a pretty brunette lying on the floor with a bullet in her head.

Phillipe: "Who is that?"

Helen: "My contact."

Phillipe: "Pack up and leave her. Meet me downstairs."

Phillipe ran down to the body that lay in the service alley. The tall man was just standing up when Phillipe came from behind and crushed his knee. He grabbed the man by his tie and punched him unconscious.

Amir's black Mercedes Benz backed in close, and the trunk opened. Phillipe tossed the man in and closed it. Helen drove away fast, with Master Chief following. Phillipe gave driving instructions into a more rural area, where Monaco's farming industry was located. As Phillipe instructed, Helen made a right turn into a cul-de-sac and stopped.

Phillipe pulled the tall man out of the trunk and administered what looked like a sedative. He picked up the man and walked down the hill about a half mile to a large tree. Behind some thick brush was a camouflage tarp. Underneath sat an old Range Rover. Phillipe tossed the man into the back and drove away. Helen said nothing because Mr. Rainbird seemed to know what he was doing.

After a few lefts and rights, they slowed down at a small warehouse. Phillipe pulled out a set of keys and unlocked the security gate. He punched in a code on the keypad, which caused a loud buzzing that allowed the metal door to open. Phillipe turned on the lights and told Helen to help with the body of the tall man. To Helen's surprise, the inside of the warehouse was a fully functional safe house with weapons, a kitchen, medical supplies, and a bathroom.

Phillipe placed the man in a metal chair that was anchored to the cement floor. Using heavy chains and padlocks, Phillipe secured the prisoner.

Phillipe: "That should do it. I'll make coffee."

Helen: "Thanks. Who do you work for?"

Phillipe: "ISA."

Helen: "Oh, I see. Why did you follow me?"

Phillipe: "Instincts."

Helen: "What did you give our new friend? I would like to have a talk with him."

Phillipe: "Basic sedative laced with LSD."

Helen: "I need him to talk. You're going to give him bloody brain damage."

Phillipe: "Calm the fuck down, Captain. I know what I'm doing. Why don't you get cleaned up, and I'll get some food working."

Helen agreed. She was filthy in more ways than one. She could deal with makeup and wig, but the stench of Amir's body all over her was repugnant.

When Helen went into the bathroom, she started to do some deductive reasoning. The tall man was butt white, which was unusual in the south of France.

Phillipe stripped the tall man's clothes off with his switchblade and found no labels or tags. He checked his hands, and they were rough. Phillipe looked inside his mouth. While looking at the back of his neck, he saw a tattoo: DIX. At first glance, Phillipe thought the guy was a fag until he remembered something he'd learned from Colonel Cohen.

Phillipe dialed a phone number and talked to Master Chief. Once hearing what Phillipe had discovered, Master Chief said he was on his way. Phillipe noticed that Helen had left her purse on the table. He reached in and retrieved her Walther.

After about twenty minutes of soaking, Helen emerged from the bathroom without the wig.

Phillipe: "Would you like some coffee, maybe something to eat?"

Helen: "Just coffee, please."

Phillipe: "Feeling better?"

Helen: "Yes, thank you. Coffee tastes good. Can you cook?"

Phillipe: "I can make a turd."

Helen: "What does that mean?"

Phillipe: "My mother always said don't worry about being a gourmet cook, just cook well enough to make a turd."

Helen: "Your mother is funny."

Phillipe: "She also taught me to ask questions, like what's in your package?"

Helen: "That's classified, and even if I knew, I couldn't tell you."

Phillipe: Who sent you on this mission?"

Helen: "What is this?"

Phillipe: "Questions, Captain, are the best way to get to know someone, remember? OK, what do you know about the tall man?"

Helen: "I've never seen him before, and why did you take his clothes off?"

Phillipe: "You're so sure of yourself, you won't even get your cute ass out of that seat and look. Because if you did, you'd see his tattoo."

Helen was beside herself. She rushed over to see what Phillipe was talking about. When she saw the tattoo, her anger was replaced with the fear and confusion.

Helen: "DIX. Diensteinheit IX, East German special

forces."

Phillipe: "Yeah, I hear they're some bad boys and they don't give those tattoos out easily. So why would they be after you, and how did he know where your safe house was?"

Helen: "I have no bloody idea. Should we wake him and find out?"

Phillipe: "We? Oh no, baby. This your barbecue. I'm just here for the Kool-Aid."

Helen's patience dwindled the more Phillipe spoke. His attitude and suggestive commentary were not only unnecessary but unproductive. She found some adrenaline in the fridge and a hypodermic needle. Using her medical expertise, she guessed-a-mated the tall man's weight and stabbed him in the heart. The tall man jumped out of the chair. Helen filled a pot with water and threw it in his face.

Helen: "Good morning. You might remember me. I'm the one you didn't kill last night. And just to make sure we don't have a misunderstanding . . ."

Helen grabbed the thumb of his left hand and broke it.

Helen: "There. Now do we understand each other? Good. What is your mission?"

The tall man squirmed to find some relief from the pain, but said nothing.

Helen: "I hear that pressure applied to a broken appendage is much more painful than breaking a new one. Is that true?"

Helen squeezed and pulled his thumb backward, and Phillipe thought to himself, "Fuck, I love this girl."

Helen: "Oh, I didn't tell you. My friend over there gave you LSD, so without proper medical attention, you will suffer brain damage. Answer my question."

The tall man probably realized that she was telling the truth.

Tall man: "My job was to retrieve a package and eliminate those responsible for stealing it."

Helen: "Who gave you this mission? Amir?"

Tall man: "No. I'm a contractor for MI6. You stole from them."

Phillipe's eye cut toward Helen to see her reaction. This was his worst-case scenario. He had risked his friends and reputation for this bitch. Helen was either a great actress or she just realized she'd been fucked over by the people she trusted. Phillipe decided to pick up the slack in the interrogation.

Phillipe: "I don't believe you, so you'll have to prove what you're saying."

Tall man: "You're American? Great. I've worked with your CIA. My name is Ian Reinhardt. Look, I defected six years ago. Call them."

Phillipe glanced over at Helen, and a tear rolled down her face.

Phillipe: "OK. Who is your European handler?"

Tall man: "I work through contacts. I'm not sure."

Phillipe: "Guess, muthafucka, before I find another window."

Tall man: "Davis. Sean Davis."

Helen: "Oh my God!"

Master Chief Tomlinson had a saying: "If you're in a world of shit and you don't know what to do, make a shit sandwich and take bite. You'll only remember the first and last bite, but you'll be out of the shit you're in."

Phillipe never knew what the fuck Master Chief was talking about until tonight. Helen Masters had taken her first bite of a soggy shit sandwich called betrayal. She had found out that she didn't know everything, and it was fucking with her ego. Phillipe had always wondered why the female ego wasn't as analyzed as the male counterpart. If a man thinks with his dick, he is ridiculed. But if a woman thinks with her purse, it somehow elevates her sophistication. Phillipe thought anything that affected one's judgment in a negative way created problems.

After the first round of interrogation, Phillipe placed earplugs into Ian's ears, then gagged and blindfolded him before asking Helen any questions.

Phillipe: "You seem very emotional. Why?"

Helen: "Why do you think?"

Phillipe: "Who is Sean Davis?"

Helen: "My supervisor. He recruited me to work for him in West Berlin."

Phillipe: "What's in the package?"

Helen: "I don't know. I was told not to open it."

Phillipe: "By whom?"

Helen: "I need time to think."

Phillipe: "Sorry, fresh out. Open the package."

Helen: Will you bloody *shut up*?"

Phillipe: "I have two theories. Mr. Davis found out you're a double agent and sent Mr. Reinhardt here to pop a cap in your ass. Or Mr. Davis broke his dick off in your ass and sent you on a false op to cover his own misdeeds. Either way, you're compromised."

After saying that, Phillipe slowly walked over to the weapons rack and reached for a rifle. Helen pulled out her Walther.

Helen: "Don't move!"

Phillipe: "Well, Captain, this is the second time in twenty-four hours you pulled a gun on me, and you're beginning to piss me off."

Helen: "I want you to listen to me. I'm not a part of this. I'll admit I had a one-night stand with Sean, but I'm not a traitor. If you want to open the package, go ahead."

Helen put the weapon on the table.

Phillipe: "Nope. You open it. And Captain, only fools refuse to change their minds when the facts change."

Phillipe abruptly walked out into the southern France darkness. Helen stood there for a moment and held back the tears of her feelings being hurt. In some ways, he was right, though extremely crude. She picked up a kitchen knife and ripped open the protective cover. What she saw did nothing to mend her shattered ego.

Phillipe walked the perimeter, not for security purposes

so much as to forgive himself for the bitter comments he had made to Helen. He heard a bird's call and returned it.

Mac and Master Chief appeared from the thick foliage.

Master Chief: "We good?"

Phillipe: "Yeah."

Mac: "You got confirmation?"

Phillipe explained what had happened inside the safe house. After listening carefully, Master Chief decided to go in and good-cop Helen.

When Master Chief stepped through the door, he saw Helen sitting at the table in total concentration. In front of her were documents and folders labeled MI6, TOP SECRET, EYES ONLY, OPERATION: FIREFLY.

Master Chief took a seat.

Helen: "Well, I have bollocksed up this entire process."

Master Chief: "Yes, you have. When Phillipe called me, I told him to shoot you in the leg and turn you over to MI6, but he said no. He wanted to talk to you first and give you a chance. Now you're sitting on your ass feeling sorry for yourself. But the past is over, and it's your call, *Captain!*"

The job of a senior noncommissioned officer, or NCO, was to provide counsel and the occasional swift kick in the ass. Helen knew Master Chief was providing the later. She picked up the kitchen knife, and with a determined focus, she snatched the blindfold, gag, and earplugs off Ian's head.

Helen: "Tell me everything you know about Sean

Davis, or I swear to God I'll cut your balls off."

     The United States Air Force pilot Lieutenant Colonel Henry Spiller was making his fifteenth flight to Baghdad, Iraq. The American defense contracting industry had several lucrative contracts with the Saddam Hussein regime, and the monthly flights were increasing due to all the political tensions in the region. Spiller was becoming bored with the uneventful routine. He once bet his copilot that he could do it in his sleep, but this trip was a little different. He had an unscheduled stop in Portugal at Lajes Field, which was situated on the small island of Terceira. Spiller's normal copilot, Scotty, had gotten reassigned, so Spiller was breaking in a newbie by the name of John Smith.

     During the eight hours of flight time, Smith gave one-word answers to everything. He was obviously not a big sharer. The landing in Portugal apparently was for an emergency piece of equipment that the Iraq government had a real hard-on to get. Spiller had met President Hussein, and the only things important to him were money and women.

     When the ground crew weighed the container, it was too heavy with all the other equipment. The C-130 would never get off the ground, so the order came down from command to remove all the other contents from the plane. Spiller had never seen or heard of a cargo flight being emptied halfway to the destination to make room for one piece of cargo.

     Typically, another flight was scheduled ASAP, but Spiller wasn't going to worry about small shit because he was six months away from retirement, and he had an airline job all sewn up.

The black container was about six feet tall and twice as long. The forklift set the container down gently inside the cargo bay. As soon as the forklift cleared, the aircraft crew went to work securing the container. Spiller had some last-minute paper work and told his mute copilot to make preparations for immediate takeoff. The power of the C-130 shook the tarmac as it left the ground.

After several hours, Mr. Smith said he had to use the head. The plane was on autopilot, and Spiller was reading a novel. Mr. Smith emerged from the head and stabbed Spiller from behind with a hypodermic to the neck. Spiller tried to resist, but Smith was a lot stronger than he looked, and eventually, Spiller succumbed to the powerful drug.

Mr. Smith went to the cargo bay and found Talia Shia completing the same task on the two other crew members. They donned their parachutes and opened the main cargo hatch. Talia attached a tracking device, and Mr. Smith took the security chains off the package. When Talia signaled OK, Smith jettisoned the package off the plane. Talia and Smith shook hands before she launched herself into the darkness.

Smith went back into the cockpit and disengaged the autopilot. He reached for the radio, dialed the emergency frequency, and screamed, "Mayday! Mayday! This is United States Air Force 039. Heavy cargo bay fire. We're down! Mayday! Mayday!"

Once Smith was finished with his Oscar-winning performance, he moved the stick forward, sending the nose of the plane down. Smith made his way to the rear platform and jumped out. The wind turbulence the plane created would have been too much for a less experienced parachutist. Mr. Smith was a member of the Israeli Sayeret Matkal, and this jump felt routine. After Smith counted to ten, he deployed the chute and activated his tracking and infrared device.

Smith was literally flying blind. The luminous dials of his compass and watch were the only light visible. His ram air parachute glided efficiently into the wind. The darkness was parted by a signal light from a small craft, and he guided the chute down until he hit the water. The crew of the small craft fished Smith out of the cold Mediterranean Sea. They gave him a blanket and some coffee. The chief of the boat informed Mr. Smith that Miss Shia and the package had been recovered, and Smith nodded while looking at the C-130 crash into the sea. Mr. Smith said a prayer in Hebrew for the crew and begged God to forgive him.

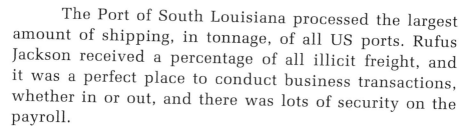

Chapter 10

The Port of South Louisiana processed the largest amount of shipping, in tonnage, of all US ports. Rufus Jackson received a percentage of all illicit freight, and it was a perfect place to conduct business transactions, whether in or out, and there was lots of security on the payroll.

A large shipment of cocaine had entered the port on its way to Chicago. Half of it would be loaded onto trucks, and the other half would be floated up the river on barges, all under the protection of Rufus Jackson.

Two unknown parties were in the process of exchanging money when someone shouted, "It's a fuckin' setup. Kill them niggas!"

A dozen shots rang out. The security teams of both parties tried to protect their principal. A stray bullet hit one principal in the neck, and then everyone opened fired, leaving no one unscathed. Danny Landon watched his brother call the FBI to report gunfire at the port. Dracula opened the car door and got in, saying, "Good work. They never saw it coming."

Danny said nothing. He just handed Dracula his payment and told Dracula someone would be in touch. Sammy approached the car with his hand on his gun, and Dracula exited the vehicle, said good night, and disappeared. The police sirens in the distance were getting closer, and the Landon brothers drove very casually to the airport.

Mr. Reinhardt's interrogation was not without incident. Helen's relentlessness and the intimidating presence of Master Chief Tomlinson certainly loosened up Reinhardt's tongue. Some of the intelligence Reinhardt provided was that Sean Davis's mistress was his contact and she lived in the old town sector of West Berlin. Obviously, this news didn't help Helen's disposition, and she took it out on Reinhardt. At one point, Master Chief had to take on the good-cop role.

While Mac walked the perimeter for security purposes, Phillipe established comms to Pinnacle. Initially, he was not happy to talk directly to Phillipe and even less happy that his senior personnel would involve themselves in a messy MI6 mole hunt. But Pinnacle knew that the only real currency in the intelligence business were favors. If he helped MI6 solve this issue, they would owe the Activity a lot of small favors or one big favor.

So, Pinnacle contacted Maxine Graves, MI6 Chief of Internal Security, who had a reputation for being a hard-assed cunt, but no one had more integrity. After being thoroughly tongue whipped for calling her at home and waking her up from a dead sleep, Pinnacle was allowed to update Maxine on the night's events.

Maxine Graves had heard great things about Helen Masters but wasn't surprised that the talented young operative had fallen for the reverse honeypot. Seduction was one of the best tools to use to compromise an individual, and by the time they knew what was going on, they were in too deep. In that regard, Helen Masters was lucky. Not that she wasn't still under suspicion, but she was in a better position to clear herself, and Maxine didn't have to use her resources.

Helen and the ISA team packed up what they needed into Master Chief's van. Mr. Reinhardt was placed unconscious in a large duffel bag and stowed in the back. Mac drove to a small private airport. He stopped at the last hangar, which housed a Pilatus PC-6 Porter. Phillipe ran over to the plane and started his preflight checks. The others loaded the cargo. Helen got into the copilot's seat and strapped in. There was no tower control, so Master Chief and Mac gave the all-clear sign. Before takeoff, Helen asked Phillipe if he knew how to fly, and he answered in the most Neanderthal voice possible, "Yes, me fly good."

Phillipe's grandfather Goya had taught everyone who wanted to learn to fly. It was his passion and his solace. At first, Helen was apprehensive, maybe even fearful, but Phillipe's technical and navigational skills were obvious. She realized why he had performed so well on the star course back at Herefort. When the silence between the two became unbearable, Helen said, "Where did you learn how to fly?"

Phillipe: "My grandfather taught me."

Helen: "Does he fly for a living?"

Phillipe: "No, he flew in World War I, RCAC."

Helen: "He sounds interesting. Is he still with us?"

Phillipe: Oh, yeah. He'll outlive us all. Your grandparents still around?"

Helen: "One died when I was young, but everyone else is fine."

The conversation ebbed and flowed until the first refueling point in Switzerland. One hour later, Phillipe and Helen headed north to Germany. When they got to cruising altitude, Phillipe let Helen take the controls. She was a natural and totally fearless. As Phillipe watched, Helen couldn't help but think of the worst-case scenario and the question of whether she was bent and could he shoot her if need be.

Luxembourg City, Luxembourg, the capital of Luxembourg, had one of the highest incomes per capita in the world because the main industry was a secret banking system that allowed anyone to deposit large sums of money without questions. Which is why it was the perfect place for the IZMENENIYE headquarters. The meeting that was taking place was for finding out what had happened to the organization's nukes, or code name Discourse.

All six members took their assigned places, and the phone rang. Member one placed the call on the speaker, and an electronic-modulated voice said, "What the fuck happened to our operation?"

Member one: "We can't be sure. It's too early to tell if we have been compromised."

Member two: "We're checking all of our CIA, MI6, and Mossad contacts, but no one is claiming responsibility."

Voice: "Do any of you know how much money this organization has lost? This is unacceptable. Now all of you have forty-eight hours to give me who is responsible! What about Operation Firefly?"

Member three: "Our man has not reported back, but it shouldn't be long."

Voice: "Good. That is all."

An electronic beep signaled that the line was clear. The members quickly moved without speaking inside of the castle to the various cars awaiting cars them. Member three entered his Mercedes Benz limousine and told the driver, "Airport!"

The driver turned and said, "Yes, Mr. Davis."

Nina Meyer walked briskly through her neighborhood of old town from the local college. She was well known and liked by everyone. Her beautiful long blonde hair was her trademark, and all the merchants in the area waved at her from half a block away. Nina's mood was especially good because the love of her life was returning from a business trip today, and they would spend the day under the warm covers. Nina had always dreamed of meeting the perfect man, one who was as successful as he was handsome. Her luxurious third-story apartment was tastefully furnished, all provided by her future husband. She opened the door of the apartment and heard music. Her heart soared until she was knocked unconscious.

Phillipe and Master Chief were searching the den/office area when Nina came to. She tried to move, but she was tied to a chair and gagged. A woman with blonde hair was the first to speak to her after removing the gag.

Helen: "Well, hello. I hope I didn't hurt you too much. Where's your boyfriend?"

Nina: "Look, I don't have much money. Just take it."

Helen slapped Nina across the face and grabbed her by the hair.

Helen: "I need you to focus on my questions. Where is your boyfriend?"

Nina: "Sean? Why do you want him? What's going on here?"

Helen punched Nina in the nose, causing blood to run down her face, and she began to cry.

Helen: "Look, bitch. I want your boyfriend, not you. Where is he?"

Nina: "On a business trip. He'll be back today."

Helen: "Did he tell you where he was going?"

Nina: He said Luxembourg. Please don't hit me again!"

Nina saw that the two black men had found Sean's safe.

Helen: "What's the combination?"

Nina didn't want say. Sean had trusted her with some very important things. That's when the blonde cunt pointed a shotgun at her knee.

Nina: "Thirty-four, twenty-four, thirty-six."

Helen: "Your measurements? How classy."

Nina: "Fuck you. Sean will kill you all!"

Phillipe felt that something was wrong. Nina was talking big, so he told Helen to make Nina open the safe. Nina's face turned pale, and she said she wouldn't do it. Helen insisted by dragging Nina to the safe.

Helen: "Now, we are going to open the safe, and any little surprises, we are all going to experience them together."

Nina: "No, no, no, no! It's booby-trapped, if you open it too far."

Master Chief went to work on the safe. One of his many skills was that he was a fully qualified Explosive Ordinance Disposal operator. Once he knew what to look for, the device was deactivated in minutes.

The contents of the safe included money and files. Phillipe found a backup pistol under the desk. He began to disassemble the 9mm Beretta pistol to shorten the firing pin, and Master Chief cleaned out the safe. After everything was done, Helen told Master Chief and Phillipe to leave. They wished her good luck and put Nina in a large chest for transport.

The ISA van in the parking lot was marked FRITZ ELECTRIC. Inside was high-tech surveillance equipment being operated by the major. After Master Chief and Phillipe took their seats, they heard Mac over the radio.

Mac: "Control, this Eagle. Copy?"

Major: "Eagle, this is Control. We copy. You in position?"

Mac: "Roger that. Got eyes on the target. Do I have a

green light. Copy?"

Major: *Negative*! Not till I give the order. Copy?"

Mac: "Yeah, I copy. I'm just fuckin' with you. Copy?"

Major: "Ha ha. Now shut the fuck the up."

Sean Davis pulled his new Mercedes into his usual parking space. When he got out of the car, he took a quick glance around to see if anything was out of the ordinary. He did notice an electrician's van at the far end of the lot, but remembered that the complex had been experiencing power outages. He was naturally paranoid, and sometimes it was a burden.

He walked out of the elevator to Nina's apartment. The first thing he noticed when he entered was how dark it was.

"Bloody hell, Nina," he shouted. He made his way to the office. He couldn't believe his eyes. The safe was open and emptied. Before he could make a phone call, he saw Nina sitting on the couch.

Sean: "Nina, what the hell is going on?"

Helen: "Sorry, Nina just left."

Sean: "Who is that?"

Helen: "Helen Masters. I don't have clearance to report to the ops center, so this is the next best thing. Yeah."

Sean: "My God, Helen. I've been looking for you. How did you get here?"

Helen: "Well, it's so wonderful to be loved, but surprising, because I heard you wanted me dead."

Sean: "No, of course not. One question: Do you know anything about my safe?"

Helen: "Yes, Nina cleaned it out after I told her about our affair. She became very upset, and being a gracious host, she invited me to stay.

Sean knew that Helen was playing a game—a very dangerous game with one of the most accomplished operatives in the world. And she had already lost; she just didn't know it yet.

Sean walked around the desk to where his backup piece was stashed.

Sean: "You know, you haven't answered my question. How did you know about this place?"

Helen: "Oh, yes. Well, the tall man who tried to kill me was very cooperative and told me all sorts of interesting things, you heartless bastard."

Sean pulled the Beretta out and cocked it.

Sean: "My dear Helen, you are not long for this business. You have too many daddy issues, and now you're going to die."

Helen: "Why? Just to cover that you're selling secrets?"

Sean: "You are naïve. I didn't sell anything. I gave Amir those documents. You are the target, and they want you dead."

Helen: "Who? Why?"

Sean: "The most powerful organization on the planet. But I don't know why, I'm sorry."

Sean aimed for Helen's head and pulled the trigger, but there was only a click. He tried to clear the weapon several times. From under the pillows of the couch emerged a 24-gauge shotgun.

Helen: "Drop the weapon now."

Sean did not hesitate and raised his hands in the air.

Helen: "Tell me more about this organization."

Sean: "I can help you only if I'm alive, and MI6 protocol is to take me in. This could be a career builder."

Helen: "So, you're not going to tell me?"

Sean: "Not like this. Take me in."

Helen: "You know, I think you were right. I do have daddy issues. You couple that with a woman scorned and my period, and I feel like I'm losing control."

Helen aimed between Sean's legs and pulled the trigger, cutting Sean in half. The top half fell to the ground. Sean tried to breathe, but the trauma had caused shock. Helen kneeled down and laid the shotgun next to him.

Helen: "You'll be dead in four minutes, so allow me to tell you what happens next. Your girlfriend, or me with a wig, will leave this apartment, and her neighbors will see her running away. The shotgun has her fingerprints on it, and the police will rule your death a crime of passion. Personally, from a jilted lover's standpoint, you are dying in the most horrible way a man can, which is vindication for me. Bye bye."

Helen ran out of the apartment screaming, to a car

stolen for just this moment. The ISA team regrouped and headed for the safe house. While en route, they picked up the brunette version of Helen Masters at a predetermined location. No one said anything about what had happened. Every man on the planet felt empathy for any man who lost his balls. It's a sacred and unspoken alliance. While at the safe house, Phillipe offered Helen a cup of coffee, and she cheerfully accepted. She could feel the tension, so she asked, "Does everyone here know what organization Sean spoke of?"

Major: "Yeah, we do. They call themselves IZMENENIYE, or the Change. A bunch of disavowed spies from different countries who came together to run financial black ops."

Master Chief: "They tried to smuggle nukes to Iran and Iraq to manipulate the oil markets. Fortunately, we stopped them."

Major: Which is why you and lover boy over there crossed paths. Amir's network was transportation contractor, and now we find out they want you dead. Why?"

Helen: "I have never heard any of this shite."

Master Chief: "Well, they heard of your ass, and these people don't play. Your family is in danger. Oh, by the way, Maxine Graves wants to meet you at the Sheraton in a hour. I suggest that you take an escort."

Helen: "OK. I'm going to need those tapes of Sean."

Phillipe: "We didn't record the last few minutes. You're covered."

Major: "If you want to get away with a crime ask, Mr. Pelican."

Phillipe: "Go to hell. Helen, I disabled your Walther."

Helen checked her weapon.

Phillipe: "I cut the firing pin."

Helen: "Prick."

Helen stood on a corner a couple of blocks away from the Sheraton. She adjusted her pantsuit and brooch to assure that her appearance was proper. She turned to look at Phillipe sitting in a 1979 Volkswagen Rabbit and talked into her brooch.

Helen: "Sound check, check."

Phillipe flashed the headlights, and Helen started walking to her meeting with the internal security chief. She knew that it could go wrong quickly. Being arrested was a best-case scenario. If Maxine Graves was a member of the Change, Helen could be assassinated as soon as she stepped through the door, or kidnapped and tortured. She knew Mac had overwatch, and Phillipe was on evac. That would give her a chance to escape.

She walked quickly through the lobby into the elevator. She a saw at least two MI6 security men, which was to be expected. The ride to the twelfth floor took an eternity. She knocked at room 1212, and a large man opened the door, waving her inside without a word. The suite was busy with activity. There was four administration personnel sorting out stacks of papers and talking on the phone.

Maxine Graves saw Helen and extended her hand

in friendship. They sat down for a cup of tea, but Helen declined.

Maxine: "I understand better than most. You're still in operation mode, and you don't know who to trust."

Helen: "Well, it has been a day."

Maxine: "Quite. Do you have the tapes and documents?"

Helen: "In my briefcase."

Maxine: "Good. My assistant will take care of everything. Now for some girl talk. Tell me about this Mr. Rainbird. From what I hear, he sounds yummy."

Helen: "I don't know what you mean."

Maxine: "Don't you? It was my understanding that he is quite fond of you."

Helen: "I wouldn't know."

Maxine: "I'm sorry, dear, but before I offer you a job, I have to know who I'm dealing with."

Helen: "Why would you do that unless you want to keep an eye on me?"

Maxine: "Young lady, you are delightfully suspicious. You will report to me in my office in three days, and together we will take down this IZMENENIYE. I hope that's satisfactory with you and everyone that's listening on your brooch radio."

Helen: "OK. I will see you in three days. Thank you."

Maxine: "Mr. Rainbird and Mr. McManus, I'm so disappointed that I didn't meet you."

Helen turned and walked out.

Mac had observed the entire meeting from an adjacent building through the scope of a high-power sniper rifle.

Mac: "Oh, yeah. You know, she's kinda hot for an old lady. Copy?"

Phillipe: "You do know she's old enough to be your mom."

Mac: "That's what makes her hot. She can cut the crust off my sandwiches any day. Copy?"

Phillipe: "Fuckin' marines. You heading to the RV?"

Mac: "That's a negative. I'll make it back. You two need to talk. Give me a call if you need a board. Copy?"

Phillipe: "What board? Copy?"

Mac: "The one you'll need to strap across your ass so you won't fall in. Out."

The Café Jazz was the most popular night spot in West Berlin, especially when a big name was in town, and tonight was no different because Herbert Hancock was on the set. His mixture of traditional and contemporary jazz, sprinkled with funk, was infectious.

Helen and Phillipe sat in the center of the club. After dinner drinks were served, Phillipe enjoyed several moments of laughter with Helen. There were other times when, looking into her eyes, Phillipe found himself in a euphoric state of mind. In between sets, he questioned

Helen's ethnicity because of her dark pigmentation. She revealed that her paternal grandmother was full-blooded Apache, and at various times in her life, she had lied and said she was Italian or Spanish.

Phillipe told her about Goya and asked if she was ashamed of her heritage. Helen admitted that she had always felt different because she was trying to fit in. She also had not seen her grandmother in more than five years. Phillipe told her that it was never too late to reconcile and start a new chapter.

Helen found herself becoming very attracted to Phillipe. He had believed in her when nobody else would, and they both had a shared a common background, so he would never judge her. Helen had a flight scheduled to leave at 11:00 p.m., but she didn't want to leave until Phillipe said, "We better leave or you'll miss your flight."

Helen grabbed her coat quickly so she wouldn't change her mind, and they both left the club with the same feeling of don't mess this up with sex. Phillipe made the ride to the airport fun by making fun of the absurdity of all that had transpired in the course of a week. He stopped at the British Airways terminal and retrieved Helen's bag.

Helen: "Well, I guess this is good-bye."

Phillipe: "For now. Besides, you're going to give me your number."

Helen: "Oh really? Why is that?"

Phillipe: "Because the Change is still out there, and it's just a matter of time before they know about all of us. We need each other."

Helen pulled out a pen and paper and wrote down her Nana's number, her contact just until she got settled in London.

Phillipe took the number and softly kissed her on the lips. He pulled her close enough to feel her heartbeat.

Phillipe: "If you need me, I will be there for you."

Helen: "OK."

Phillipe returned to the car and left. Helen stood there for a moment, then realized she was staring before she entered the terminal.

Detectives Adam Canaby and Joe Barnes had sat in an unmarked police van for the last couple of months. They had been getting anonymous tips about kingpin Rufus Jackson's deals all over the city. Of course, nothing ever tied directly to him, but the information had been great—clean and precise. This made Canaby nervous because usually street information came from unreliable sources. But this shit seemed professional—dates, times, places, and manpower.

The large Conex truck moved slowly, with the security cars front and back, into a warehouse in the valley. Before they could close the loading dock doors, several teams of narcotics officers and SWAT descended upon the Nahlense crews. The Nahlense guys opened fire on the police officers, and a gun battle ensued for ten minutes. In total, there were three wounded and seven dead along with a truckload of various drugs. A clean bust—too clean. Canaby felt he was being used for somebody's personal bullshit agenda, and Canaby was tired of playing catch up.

Canaby, Barnes, and the police department were all pawns on a chessboard, with only one real player. Rainbird.

THE END AND THE JUST THE BEGINNING

CPSIA information can be obtained
at www.ICGtesting.com
Printed in the USA
LVOW05s0413230617
539110LV00030B/1085/P